I0784449

CONTENT WARNING

This novel contains brief, explicit scenes of the domestic violence.
It also includes murder and dismemberment. Please read with care.

This book is a work of fiction. Any reference to historical events, real people, or real places are used fictitiously. Other names, characters, places, and events are products of the author's or artists imagination, and any resemblance to actual events or places or persons, living or dead, is entirely coincidental.

Book Design and Layout by Russell Shuler + Project13.com

Cover Design by Richard Norris at Project13.com

CON FESS IONS

FROM THE CHAIR

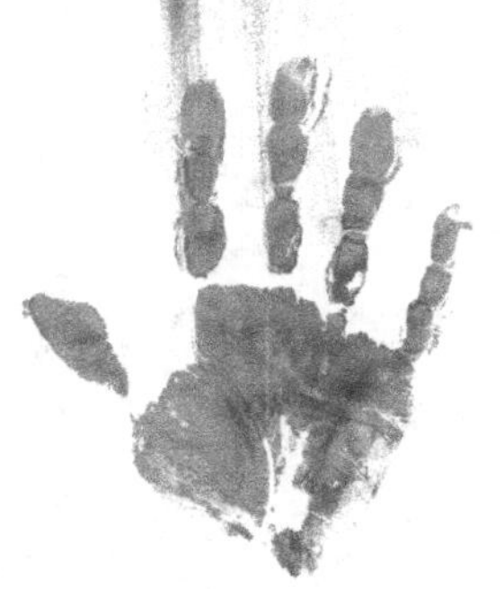

E
F

PLANTING THE DEMON SEED

CHAPTER 1

The evening air outside the trailer was cooling down from another scorcher. A gentle breeze swept across the pasture while the soft sounds of cows mooing in the field supplied a nice bass line to the cicada's high-pitched trill. A pack of coyotes, a.k.a. "Song Dogs," bayed in the distance. The moon was the kind Emmylou Harris might sing about as a bunch of cowboys sit around the campfire eating beans and breaking wind.

For the next several hours, the girls worked methodically and intensely. Jesse kicked on some heavy metal tunes, rocking and swaying to the beat while she hacked and sawed. There was a fire in her eyes that Sana had never seen before, and once again, she was glad to know Jesse was on her team.

The overhead LEDs lit up the inside of the trailer, throwing everything not lit directly into harsh shadows. Knives, cleavers, and saw blades of every description hung on long magnetic strips just above the counter. Jesse kept the saws and other power tools stored in the deep pull-out drawers below the counter-top area—a place for everything, and everything in its place.

Raw blood and other body fluids swirled aimlessly around the shallow stainless-steel sink to the right and drained into a holding tank below.

They had tucked the heads, hands, and feet away in plastic barrels filled with a salty brine mixture, to be processed later into animal feed.

A high-pressure spray nozzle was neatly coiled at the end of the trailer, making it easy to hose down the entire trailer interior when needed.

The baby had been overly active, but Sana had grown used to that. It seemed to enjoy the carnage as much as Jesse did, maybe more.

They had almost finished processing the second lackey. Sana had made all the heavy cuts, so it was a matter of trimming some fat here and rib cartilage there, wrapping it all up, and they'd be good to go. Nate and the first lackey were already wrapped and stored in the freezer. All in all, an excellent yield. Kim Chee would be so excited.

Stepping back so she could survey the counter, Jesse noticed something alarming, and turned to Sana and motioned for her to stop.

"Whoa, girl! Holy shit, you've got a lot of blood running down your legs there! You've got to be more careful not to get that shit on you. There's no telling what kind of germs these crazy fuckers might be carrying."

Sana powered down her saw, flipped her blood-spattered face mask up, looked down at her thighs, and realized the bloody mess was coming from her, not the body on the counter. She hiked up her work apron, looked more closely, and saw a mixture of sticky fluid and fresh blood.

"What the... Oh shit, that's coming from me! Oh no, I think my water just broke!"

Then, as if she'd flipped the main switch on a power station, she started cramping for all she was worth. She staggered back against the trailer wall in pain and slid down to the floor.

"Oh my God! I think this little devil is gonna make his appearance tonight. What the fuck are we going to do?"

(NINE MONTHS EARLIER)

It was a cold and miserably rainy night, just after closing time at the local watering hole. Sana and her mom were headed home when their piece-of-shit beater of a car ran out of gas. Sana drove while Tara was passed out drunk in the back seat, which was her everyday existence.

"No, no, no! This can't be happening. Hell-to-the-no, no, no! Not out here in the middle of no-fucking-where," Sana yelled.

Somehow, she managed to get the car off the highway and onto the shoulder. She flipped on the emergency blinkers and waited for the rain to subside, hoping she could rouse her mom out of her drunken stupor and walk the few miles back to the trailer by then.

The rain continued to pour and showed no signs of clearing soon. The wet road absorbed the little light that crept through the clouds and looked like a jet-black river. Fat raindrops echoed off the car's roof like someone was steadily hitting it with a ball-peen hammer.

A few cars passed, but no one stopped.

And, of course, no highway patrols were cruising the area at this time of night—you only ran into them when you could least afford to do so.

Jeff was headed home after a long shift at the steel mill, where he worked as a production-line welder. He sported his obligatory red MAGA hat, and Fox News blared on his radio. The water hissed off the tires of his massive RAM dually as the Cummins diesel purred at an even 1,200 rpm.

He had the window cracked just enough to spit from his cheek full of chewing tobacco, which left a trail of brown streaks down the side of the truck that looked like someone had thrown a shit grenade at him. The black and blue upside-down American flag mounted on the fifth wheel in the truck bed completed the tableau.

He saw the emergency flashers blinking ahead in the darkness as he crested the hilltop.

Who the hell's out here at this time of night?

He decided to stop and see what was up. And when he saw it was a pretty young black girl sitting behind the wheel, looking scared and alone, he knew it was his lucky day.

Jeff slowly rolled past the car and pulled over onto the shoulder. He put on his emergency blinkers, checked his cap in the mirror, and exited the vehicle, leaving the big diesel running.

The rain pelted him as he slowly walked towards the car. All Sana could see through the rain-spattered windshield was his long-legged, blinking silhouette moving across the dark profile of the truck.

The taillights from the truck and the drizzling water drops created what she thought would have been a beautiful abstract image on the windshield—a study in red, orange, and black.

Jeff stopped just outside the driver's side window and waited, standing there, for an uncomfortably long time before bending down so she could see his face. The red-orange light of the flashers made his already menacing countenance look even more so. Sana thought the rain that ran down his face looked like fresh blood.

"Hey! Looks like you could use a bit of an assist. What's the problem?"

Jeff said, talking through the still-closed window.

Then, as if to punctuate his question, he turned his head and spit a nasty wad of tobacco juice on the side of the car.

"We ran out of gas and need a ride back to town. My mom's in the back," Sana said through the slightly cracked window.

Upon hearing this, Tara moaned loudly and rolled over on the seat.

"Don't suppose you have a gas can in back of that big ol' rig of yours?" she asked as kindly as her trembling voice could manage.

"That'd be a no, sugar, as that big ol' truck of mine runs on diesel, not gas," Jeff replied sarcastically. Then he stood up, looked around, and said, "Tell you what, since it's raining cats and fuckin' dogs out here, I'll do you a solid and give you and your mom a lift. We can sort out the rest later. How's that sound?"

"Okay, okay! That'd be great. Can you help me get her out of the back and into your truck?"

At this point, Sana's fight-or-flight response should have kicked into high gear, or at a minimum, made alarm bells go off. But living through years of domestic violence abuse had stunted her evolutionary growth, so instead, she continued to do as Jeff asked, trusting him implicitly.

"Sure, sugar. Just unlock the doors, and we can get her out," Jeff said, grinning with evil pride.

They struggled together to extract Tara from the car's back seat and, draping her arms across their shoulders, walked her dead weight to Jeff's waiting truck. Hearing the radio still blaring Fox News as she opened the door, Sana got in first and practically had to drag her mom up and into the truck as Jeff pushed her from behind, groping her freely as he did so. Then, he shut the door behind her and slowly walked across the front of the truck as the headlight beams revealed his sinister face to Sana.

"Which way's home?" Jeff asked as he hopped in behind the wheel.

Sana gave him the address as best she could. Since their home was out in the country on a rural dirt road, this involved a lot of hand gestures, saying a turn at a highway such and such, and then he'd see the trailer set back against the woods. Jeff slowly grinned at all this, and they were off. They rode silently, the only break coming when Sana said, "Turn here," or "It's the next right." Finally, the trailer was in sight, and Sana felt relieved they had made it home safely.

Jeff rolled his big truck close to the trailer's front door and stopped. Then, he quickly turned to Sana, seated next to him, reached over, roughly grabbed her by the arm, and dragged her out of the truck. She struggled halfheartedly against him but didn't dare scream or put up too much of a fight, as she instinctively knew what that would lead to. He shoved her through the trailer's front door onto the seedy sofa waiting inside. Then, he knocked her unconscious with an unexpected punch to the side of her jaw. This seeming act of kindness on his part helped her better deal with the ensuing rape that followed for her and her mother.

After the rape, Jeff disappeared into the still-rainy night, but not before he ransacked their trailer, looking for anything valuable or something he might keep as a trophy.

When they regained consciousness a while later, they wondered how badly he had molested them. Tara took it as just another lousy day in a lifetime of bad days. Sana, on the other hand, was utterly devastated. A couple of months later, when her teenage breasts began to feel extremely sensitive and her period was late, she knew things would only worsen. She had to get help, but she didn't know precisely how to go about that.

She called the free clinic and set a time to stop by for a check-up. As expected, they confirmed her worst fears—she was pregnant with this horrible man's baby resulting from the brutal rape.

Tara, who had been down this very road before, told her to go to the

Social Services office and see what help they might have. The worst that could happen is that there would be no help, but they might surprise her and be able to give her some options.

The Social Services office was downtown, part of a large government complex of buildings and green spaces. The area made Sana nervous just by being there. She didn't like all the imposing columns and stone walls. The security check-ins. Electric locks on every door. It all made her feel insignificant and suspect.

Sana finally arrived at the Social Services office and checked in with the receptionist behind the counter.

Fliers for a variety of services covered the walls, from free income tax preparation to domestic violence abuse counseling to sign-up assistance for Healthcare.gov. A fake ficus tree stood in the corner, covered with years of dust. Muzak® played through a crackly speaker overhead.

When her representative, Delores, called her back to her office to meet, things didn't improve much. Her desk was piled high with what Sana assumed were ongoing case files. The "In" and "Out" boxes overflowed on one desk corner. The only bright spot was the *Hang in there* poster with a little kitten hanging by a thread off a sofa.

Sana followed Delores down the hall to a small conference room outfitted with various cameras and microphones. The room was bare otherwise. They hadn't tried to make it feel inviting, calming, or anything other than depressing. The institutional beige paint and stained acoustic ceiling tiles only added to the despair.

After some brief pleasantries and explanations of what was about to happen, Delores asked Sana if she had reported the incident to the authorities, knowing full well what the answer would be.

"No."

This question was followed by another almost as evident as the first:

"Do you know the person who did this to you?"

Again, "No."

"All I know is he's young, white, and drives one of those big-ass dually-diesel trucks with a upside-down American flag flying in the back. And he wore one of those red MAGA hats like you always see on the TV. He's a scary-ass dude," Sana said, embarrassed at what she let slip.

Upon hearing this, Delores cringed visibly. She scribbled some notes in Sana's record and left the room, saying, "I'll be right back. Just sit tight for a few minutes, please."

Delores returned to her desk and thought about the next steps. She wanted to help Sana for several reasons.

First, her job was to help clients through these kinds of situations.

But more than that, she had grown up with Sana's mom and knew her background better than most. She had seen her go down the wrong path early on and never seemed able to return to a better road. And now her daughter was in danger of making precisely the same mistake. She felt there had to be a way to correct this or, at a minimum, improve the situation.

She picked up the phone and called the sheriff. She had established a cordial working relationship with the new lady sheriff, a first in these parts and a Black woman. She would hypothetically talk through Sana's case and see what options might be available.

"Hey, Sheriff. Thanks for taking my call. Delores Singletary over at Social Services. I have a tough case I'd like to run past you. Do you have a minute to spare?" Delores asked.

"Well, hello, Delores. It's good to hear from you. I'll certainly help if I can. What do you have for me?" the sheriff replied.

Delores quickly took her through the information she had gathered, omitting personal connections, and awaited the sheriff's response. Her reply was way more than she had ever dreamed of.

"I think I know the person you're looking for, even from this sketchy description, but I need you to ask your 'hypothetical client' one question for me. Ask her if this guy spits chewing tobacco."

Delores wrote the request down quickly and thanked the sheriff for her help. She'd be back in touch once she had an answer for her.

"Be careful, Delores. If the answer is 'Yes,' we are dealing with a truly evil and dangerous person," the sheriff added before she could hang up.

Delores re-entered the intake room.

"Okay, I've spoken to some others about your case, and they have a question for you that will help possibly identify the person. Did he chew or spit tobacco?"

Sana closed her eyes and recalled the scene outside the car window of Jeff as he first approached the car.

"Yeah, yeah, I think so. When we ran out of gas that night, he stopped and offered to help. He spoke to me through the car window, then turned and spit on our car door. At first, I thought he'd spit on the ground, then I saw later it was all down the side of our car. Asshole."

"Thank you for answering that question for me. That will help us decide the next steps. I'll keep you informed as best I can, and we may need to get together to ask some additional questions. Would that be okay?" Delores asked as she quickly wrote down her response and proceeded to wrap things up with Sana.

"You know, I don' want to cause nobody any trouble. I jus' wanted to see if there might be some help once this baby arrives. I can't depend on Mom for anything much," Sana replied hesitantly.

This exchange saddened Delores greatly, and she said, "Sana, honey, I know your mom. She and I grew up together. I was there when we all saw her go down the wrong path—making bad choices and falling in with the wrong crowd. She never made it back out of the mess she created. I don't want to see the same thing happen to you, so when I call you, and I WILL call you, please answer the phone. We are going to help you. Okay?"

"Oh! Okay. Thank you," Sana replied, looking shocked.

CHAPTER 2

The concertina wire along the top of the fence surrounding the prison shimmered in the bright daylight. Monotone announcements echoed across the compound from several tower-mounted loudspeakers. Two teams of inmates played basketball on a broken concrete pad; one team wore shirts, the other skins. Others worked out with makeshift weight benches, while others loitered in groups selling contraband and playing cards. The guards in the pen listened and learned what they could, knowing they might want some of what was available later. Guards in the towers kept watch with long guns ready.

"Alright, convict, you've got ten minutes. Understood?" the guard asked as the old white cracker of a man entered the visitation room.

His prison tattoos, crew-cut hair, and ever-present toothpick sticking out of his mouth tried their best to make him appear threatening, but only made him look like an old fool.

He nodded, slowly walked to his assigned booth slot, sat before the scratched-up plexiglass, and stared at his son Jeff on the other side.

They picked up their respective handsets, and as was always the case, there was no tender "How are you doing? You look good." kind of prattle, just the beginnings of a harsh interrogation from the crusty old fuck in the orange jumpsuit.

"I hear sales on the street have been off since I got slammed here. What do you have to say for yourself, boy?" asked the father. "I'm depending on you to move this shit while I'm locked away in here, so don't you go gettin' all sideways on me."

Trying his best to burn holes through his father's skull with his eyes, Jeff said, "Shit is sideways because you got your ass all holed up in here. The Po-Po is watching me night and day like a god-danged hawk. Why the hell? I can't take a shit that they don't know whether it floated or not, so step back off this line of bullshit."

The crusty old fuck laughed and then leaned in towards the glass.

"Looks like someone is trying to reach puberty. 'Bout damn time don't you think?," the father said, flashing his son a menacing smile.

"Aww, fuck you, old man! I didn't come here to get all lectured up on what you think I should be doing. I'm taking care of business as best I can. Don't worry your tight little jail-house ass; when the shit cools off a bit, I'm going to move some product. You just need to keep that crooked nose of yours clean for the next six months, and maybe, just maybe, you can get the hell out of here," Jeff replied.

"Well then, since you have everything under control, I guess I'll be on my merry way then. Tell your Ma, I said, 'Hey!' next time you see her."

Then, laughing a little too loudly, he slid his chair back and hung up the phone.

At this, Jeff yelled as he jumped up, kicked his chair over, and pounded on the glass.

"You son of a bitch! It's a damned good thing you're in there and not out here, or you'd be a dead man!"

The guards quickly grabbed Jeff by the shoulders and slammed him down roughly in his chair as his father walked away on the other side of the glass, laughing as the door slammed behind him.

As he walked back down the depressing hallways to leave the prison, Jeff recalled how his mother and father were constantly at each other's throats.

First, he'd come home three sheets to the wind after a long night of hard drinking, and she'd start nagging him about pissing all his money away.

Then, to return the favor, he'd climb all over her ass about how the house was always a mess and why in the hell didn't she get a job if she was so damned concerned about money?

Finally, the abusive tornado would spiral up and out of control until one or the other threw something, either a punch or an empty liquor bottle.

But things with his dad had taken a very different turn the last time he saw his mother.

Nate, a slime-ball character of the first order, had suckered his father into being part of his gang, and they started selling bootleg fentanyl and other illegal drugs on the street. Suddenly, he was flush with cash, and the whiny wife wanted to know certain things that, looking back, would have been better left a mystery. So, he shared his newfound business enterprise with her. Lacking any self-control or common sense of the standard variety, his wife begged him to let her try some of this stuff. At first, he said, "No, that's not a good idea." But after she continued to whine and bitch at him, his thinking turned around, and he felt it might just be the best idea she'd had lately.

"Okay, okay, but you need to know one thing: this shit is potent. If you fool with too much of it, you're a goner, you hear me, so listen when I tell you, be careful," he said.

He pulled a small bag out of his pocket and, with great care, carefully formed a line of cocaine laced with fentanyl on a nasty mirror for her.

She stared at it like it was the greatest gift she had ever received.

"Oh yeah, that's what I'm talking about!"

Then she quickly rolled a filthy dollar bill up and took one long snort across the mirror.

"Hoo-wee! This shit is the bomb!" she said, quickly wiping her nose and licking her hand.

"Listen to what I'm telling you; this is not like other drugs. You mess with this stuff, and you'll be gone before you know it. So, when it hits you and you start feeling better than you've ever felt in your life, don't go thinking twice as much will be twice as good. Got it?" he growled.

"Yeah, I got it," she whined, already starting to feel the effects.

It wasn't long before she passed out on the sofa, and the father could enjoy quiet for the first time in a long while.

After a bit, he looked over at her. *You know, when she isn't running that danged mouth of hers like she's gettin' paid by the word, she ain't too bad on the eyes.*

So, he reached over and rubbed her suggestively between her legs, and she moaned with what he took as a sign of permission. Then he let his little head take over the decision-making, dropped his pants, and climbed on top of her. He was just about to get happy with it when she rousted herself out of her stupor, started squirming, and tried to fight him off.

"What the fuck are you doing? Settle your stupid ass down, you crazy bitch!" he screamed.

"Get off me, you fucking asshole!" she screamed back and took a swing at him. But in her wasted state, she missed the mark entirely. His punch, however, made contact right in her left eye, knocking her out.

"Seems you always want to take the hard road. One day, you'll learn where that road leads," he said to her inert body, having regained control.

Then he continued as he saw fit and, when finished, rolled her off the sofa onto her back, lying on the floor with her pants still pulled down.

Shortly after, he grabbed his keys and left the house, wasting less than a glance in her general direction. When he returned a few hours later, she was still lying there, passed out on the floor. He walked over to check on her and even considered having another go at her when he realized something was different—she had vomited while he was out and choked to death. Not good. Not good at all.

"Oh shit! What in the hell am I going to do with you now, you crazy bitch?" he screamed, tearing at his hair as if that might solve this insane scenario. Then, he quickly gathered up his belongings and took off for anywhere but there, thinking the highway might be his best choice.

Five days later, a neighbor called the police when they hadn't seen any movement at the house for some time. When they finally broke in, they found her a liquefied mess on the floor, with flies swarming all around. Even in that state of decay, the coroner felt they were dealing with a fentanyl overdose. They had seen this particular movie far too many times. So, they tagged her, bagged her, and went about notifying any next of kin. It didn't take long for them to track Jeff down.

CHAPTER 3

The cafe was bustling as Delores and the sheriff met over coffee to discuss Sana and Tara's situation. The sheriff had to admit that the smell of freshly brewed coffee and sticky buns made her mouth water.

The news that their assailant chewed tobacco confirmed in the sheriff's mind that Jeff was their man. She'd had run-ins with him and his father before, so everything Sana had told them lined up perfectly. Jeff's mother had OD'd on Fentanyl, which was the prevailing story—a story the sheriff still wasn't completely sold on. His father had disappeared after that, only to reemerge a few months later as part of a more prominent drug gang. He was never the brightest bulb in the box and got arrested when the police raided the gang's warehouse, confiscating the biggest bust to date of illegal drugs. He was, for now, safely locked away in the state pen. Jeff was lucky, though, and didn't get caught up in the raid, and word on the street was that he had taken over the business where his father had left off.

"So how do we play this with Jeff? Do you bring him in and have Sana ID him, or just arrest and charge him?" Delores asked.

The sheriff wiped her mouth after finishing a nice piece of sticky bun.

"It's not quite that simple. First, Sana would have to press charges, and so far, she's been unwilling to do that. We could use DNA to prove Jeff is the father of Sana's baby, but even that doesn't help much. If Jeff is in jail, he can't take care of his obligation to Sana and his child, so we need to figure out a way to hold him accountable some other way," the sheriff replied.

"Well, you could always arrange a shotgun wedding, or in this case, an AR-15 wedding," Delores joked.

"Ha! Don't think me crazy just yet, but I was thinking something very much along those lines. Hear me out."

Delores looked at her, stunned. She picked up her coffee, took a sip, and warmed her hands on the cup while waiting for the next shoe to drop.

"We'll put together a prenup if you will. In it, Jeff must acknowledge that he's the father. Then, we outline what's required for him to meet his obligations to Sana and the child. But, of course, all this is contingent on him staying out of trouble and off our radar. If he slips up even once, the whole case shifts, and he's on the hook for rape and all that entails."

"And you think Sana should go for something like that? Personally, I'd call you crazy just for bringing the whole idea up, but hey, that's me."

"Jeff doesn't want to get thrown in jail where his old man is already serving time. He hates that man with a passion and blames him for his mother's death. Truth be told, I'm right there with him on that. They'd tear each other apart on day one. Add to this little drama that he's as arrogant as the day is long. He'd feel like he pulled a fast one on us and signed on to prove just how smart he was."

Delores sat her cup down, leaned over, and spoke in a lowered voice.

"Like you said, I can see where he might be arrogant enough to do that, but you seem to forget he's a very dangerous man. What if he beats, or worse yet, kills, Sana and her unborn baby on the first day? I don't want that on my conscience, do you?"

"No, I don't want that either, but here's what I think: this deal is just a different kind of sentence for him to serve. The upside is that he can do his business if he keeps his nose clean. But, on the other hand, he knows the downside, and I feel that would be a good deterrent for him."

"So, what's next? We talk with Sana and her mom?" Delores asked.

"Yes. And if they're receptive to the plan, we'll draw it all up and confront Jeff," the sheriff said with a look that betrayed her misgivings.

She folded her napkin, picked up the check, and slid out of the booth.

CHAPTER 4

As they pulled to a stop at the end of the dirt drive that led to Sana and Tara's trailer, the sheriff and Delores looked at each other in utter astonishment. This trailer would have "Condemned" notices plastered everywhere in any ordinary world. Weeds had grown up around the perimeter of the trailer, so tall that they blocked the windows. A dark black grime resembling mold covered most of the remaining sun-bleached aluminum siding. Huge batts of insulation had been dragged down and out from under the trailer and left to gather dust in the yard. Trash of every description created a semi-circle, equivalent to Tara's arm strength, around the front door and out into the yard. Even the few scraggly trees that remained upright were dead.

Once they got out of the car, the scene was even more disgusting, as they noticed a small pond of raw sewage had seeped out from under the trailer, and the smell was overwhelming. The sound of buzzing flies grew louder with each step towards the trailer.

The sheriff knocked on the door and heard movement from within. Sana opened the door and silently invited them in.

The interior was dark and close, and the smell of stale tobacco smoke and liquor covered them like a dragon's breath. Sana and Tara sat on the seedy sofa across from the sheriff and Delores, who had pulled up chairs in the middle of their sad living room. A broken mirror spanned the length of the sofa above their heads. A deep layer of filth and despair covered every surface.

As Delores took a quick survey of the room, she did a double-take as she saw the sewage-covered ground through a large hole in the floor, just to the left of their refrigerator. The sound of thousands of flies filled her ears.

Internally, she almost felt sorry for Jeff and his possibly being tied in some way to this unfortunate situation, even though he was a brutal rapist and white supremacist.

Tara spoke first. "Sheriff, it's been a minute since we've seen each other. Seems like you're doing pretty well for yourself. So, what brings you out on this fine day?"

"Yes, Tara, it has been a while, and yes, I am doing okay, thank you. We're here to see if we can help you and your daughter with the situation you've found yourselves in," the sheriff replied.

Tara smiled menacingly at the sheriff, showing off her gold teeth. Sana had told her mother about the ordeal they'd experienced that night, and she'd immediately known who their assailant was.

"That would be the 'Jeff situation,' no doubt. So, what you think you gonna to do about that boy? He's bad, for damn sure, but he's also whiter than a soda cracker, and last time I checked, that trumped any card I might want to throw down."

"I could not agree more. You were always smart, Tara, even if you didn't think so. But that no-account boy and his even more no-account father have put themselves in a world of hurt. The father is in the state pen now, serving a 2-year sentence for selling fentanyl and other drugs. Jeff has been on our radar since then, and he knows one slip could land him right there with his old man, and trust me when I tell you, he hates his old man with a passion. He blames his father for his mother's death, even though we have no evidence to support that, other than she OD'd on fentanyl-laced cocaine. Sana's description of what happened to you both is terrible, and we want to see some accountability occur. But bringing him in on a rape charge would be a trying ordeal for everyone without guaranteed success. Proving his paternity would be easy enough with a DNA test, but even that doesn't help much, as he could ignore any ruling to pay child support and whatnot and take his chances with you and the courts pursuing him."

"So, what exactly can we do? Sounds like no matter where we look, there's no solution. The system and this fucker screw us over," Sana said.

Delores replied, "Sadly, the legal system is not working in your favor, but we have a potential solution to discuss. I'll admit it's a very unorthodox plan, but if we can make it work, it might provide at least some justice and, at a minimum, support for you and your unborn baby. Just hear us out before you make up your mind."

The sheriff picked up on Delores's opening.

"We've been discussing bringing Jeff to task for his actions. Believe it or not, there used to be a law on the books called 'Marry-your-rapist' that did pretty much what we we're trying to achieve with this plan. And the way things are going politically today, we might have that law again if all those evangelicals get their way. But, as we know it today, that law isn't a real solution. And bringing rape charges against him would only make his life uncomfortable. But if we bring his no-account father into the conversation with the threat of tying him to his old man, we feel that would give us some leverage. We suggest a shotgun wedding between Jeff and Sana, whereby he assumes all legal responsibilities for you and his baby. You wouldn't have to live together, and he would have very limited visitation rights, but otherwise, you're tied together legally. He'd have to provide you and the baby with a place to live. You'd have the freedom to get a job and try and move on with your life as a married woman," the sheriff said.

Sana's mouth dropped open in surprise, and her mother shook her head. Neither spoke.

"We'll meet with Jeff and tell him we know about what he did to the two of you and that we can make his life complicated and possibly reunite him with his father in prison if he doesn't play ball. But we want him to own his actions and make things easier for you and his baby, so we propose he and Sana get married in exchange for not pressing rape charges. Like you, he'd be free to go about his life as he sees fit, only as a married man with obligations. Acknowledging his involvement with his father's drug trade, even vaguely, should get his undivided attention," the sheriff continued.

"And what if *I* don't want to play along with this crazy ass idea?" Sana finally asked.

"Let's get real here for a minute. You don't have any options at this point that would even hint at a solution. Too much time has passed for you to get an abortion, plus you haven't pressed charges for the rape. And your prospects on your own are minimal and will become even less so when the baby arrives. So, we must get creative—maybe even a little crazy, as you call it—because that's where we are," the sheriff said.

Delores stepped into the fray and said, "We'll keep him on a very short leash with weekly check-ins and supervised visitation. We'll immediately bring him in if we see any signs of abuse or violent threats against you."

"So, you think you're gonna blackmail this cracker into marrying my daughter just to save his own ass? He'd be a damn fool to do something like that," Tara said.

The sheriff hung her head briefly and then looked Tara in the eye. "Okay, Tara, I'm gonna give you some tough love now, so I'll apologize for upsetting you before I start. How often have you made an even worse decision just to make it through the day? Look around here; this is no way to live, and you know it. Hell, Animal Control wouldn't let a stray dog live in such conditions as this. So, considering all that, why wouldn't Jeff make a much better choice to save his cracker ass, as you call it?"

Tara turned away from the sheriff and stared out the dirty window.

As much as she hated to admit it, the sheriff was right.

As a young child, she had fallen in with the wrong crowd in middle school, feeling it was way cooler and easier to "hang out" smoking in the bathrooms or under the bleachers than studying anything in a stupid book or going to boring classes.

And upon reaching puberty, boys' allure was far more potent than any self-control she might have had. They wanted to do "the sex thing" with her, and once she broke that seal, she also wanted them to do things with her. She quickly learned she could place a value on these things and discovered they were more than willing to pay for such pleasures. At first, these tiny pleasures were enjoyable, and the money could not have been easier to make, but once her reputation as a bona fide hooker got around, things took a severe turn.

Strangers showed up one day and offered her money in exchange for a good time. And these guys had a fast car, cigarettes, and liquor, so why not expand her horizons? But she soon realized these strangers were much more interested in raping and beating her senseless as part of their "turf discussion" in their sex trade than having a good time. This lesson about the invisible boundaries of pimps and their working gals was undoubtedly painful, but she learned it well, unlike most lessons. Dropping out of school and throwing her lot in with one of these characters seemed safer. However, this perceived safety quickly ran its course when she got pregnant with Sana, as no pimp wanted a pregnant hooker in his stable, even though specific clientele loved banging a pregnant girl.

Sana spoke up for her mother: "She tries; I swear she tries. But you know how hard it is to have no skills or education. Sitting on a bar stool and picking up John's is about the only game she can play, and we all know how rough that can be."

Delores said, "Sana, you deserve better than this." Looking around the trailer, she followed, "Pardon me for saying it, but anyone deserves better than this. While it may seem ridiculous and dangerous, this option is a way out of this nightmare. If you think it's hard now with the two of you, think how it will be when there's a new baby. And even if you give the baby up for adoption, you still must carry it to term, and that will be no picnic. So, sadly, it's one of those cases of 'Damned if you do, and damned if you don't, so hurry up and decide.' You can see that, right?"

"And what if Jeff says, 'No fuckin' way!' Then what?" Tara asked.

"We'll cross that bridge when and if we get there. So, you're good with us at least pursuing it with Jeff?" the sheriff asked.

"Seems to me like we don't have any real choice. It hurts me to say it, but you're right about livin' here. Even a bad situation with Jeff would be a step up, so let's roll the dice and see what happens," Sana said.

"Okay, we're agreed then. We'll go ahead, and I'll be in touch after the meeting with Jeff. Cross your fingers and take care of yourselves as best you can," the sheriff said.

The sheriff and Delores thanked them for their time and returned to the car. Once inside, they solemnly turned to each other and let the silence fill the conversation.

CHAPTER 5

Inside the steel mill, it was scorching hot and extremely loud. When operators lowered the giant electrode into the crucible filled with crushed cars and other recycled material, it sounded like a continuous thunderstorm raging. The massive arc of electricity that jumped from the electrode to the surface of the crucible turned everything in its path into molten metal. Sparks flew from within, and the air smelled of ozone.

Other workers who weren't actively involved in maneuvering the giant crucible stood well away from the operation, as the white-hot metal would burn away whatever it touched.

Further down the production line, workers filled vast molds of every description with molten iron. As the crucible tipped over, the white-hot metal flowed into the molds and quickly turned a fiery red. These workers, dressed in full-body heat suits to keep from burning up, directed the flow.

The fabrication and finishing of steel components, like trusses and beams, occurred in another area of the plant.

The group foreman threw the welding mask back on his head and yelled down the line of workers, "Jeff, dammit, get your worthless ass moving. The whole line is waiting for you to finish your section. You're costing us all money, so pick up the damn pace!"

Working at the steel mill was a challenge, and the fact that he was part of a team and got paid for what the group produced meant each member depended on all the others for their livelihood. They had weekly quotas to meet, which was relatively easy, but they also had incentives built in, where any production above their quota was extra cash straight into their pockets. So, if every team member worked their asses off, they could make a lot of money. But as was the case with Jeff, if you had a team member who didn't hustle or just wasn't up to the task, the other members lost money, and, in turn, they made that person's life a living hell.

"Aw, fuck off! I'm workin' as fast as I can. You don't want me to fuck this up, do you? Just gimme a sec," Jeff yelled through his welder's hat.

Then, the foreman noticed the sheriff walking onto the plant floor, heading in his direction. *What the hell? This can't be good.*

A loud alarm sounded in the distance, and flashing yellow lights spun throughout the area.

He stepped away from the production line and greeted the sheriff. He asked as politely as he could, "Can I help you?"

"I'm sorry just to show up unannounced, but I need to speak with one of your employees there, Jeff. Can you spare him for a few minutes?" the sheriff asked.

Knowing this delay would really piss off the rest of his group, he was inclined to say "no" but, using better judgment, yelled out, "Jeff, you've got a visitor. Make it quick."

When Jeff rocked his welder's mask back and saw who was waiting for him, he did a mild freak. "What the... Oh, okay. I'll be right there."

Putting his gear down and pulling off his gloves and apron, he quickly tried to figure out what the hell the sheriff might be after. Knowing it could be any number of things truly didn't help his case.

"Jeff let's step outside so we can talk freely," the sheriff said.

Once outside, Jeff thought he would try to intimidate the sheriff with his usual bluster.

"So, what the hell you doin' just showin' up here like this? I ain't done nothin' wrong, or you'd want to do a lot more than talk. You makin' me look bad in front of my people," Jeff said.

The sheriff replied sarcastically, "Well, thank you for asking such a good question, Jeff. I appreciate your willingness to engage so freely with me. I'm here to talk about your little experience with Sana and her mother a while back. They were stranded on the side of the road one rainy night after their car ran out of gas, and like a knight in shining armor, you happened along and offered to help them out of a bind."

Jeff thought for a minute, trying to figure out his best path forward.

"Oh yeah, I remember that. It was rainin' like a mutha, and their piece-of-shit car had run out of gas, so I offered them a ride home. I dropped 'em off, and that was that."

"Well, you're partly right there, Jeff. You were kind and offered them a ride home, and you did leave after that, but not before you knocked Sana out and raped her and her mother. Now that I've refreshed your memory, does that part ring a bell?"

"Now, just hold on a dang minute! I don't know what kind of crack you're on, lady, but that absolutely did not happen. No way! You've got no proof, just a couple of wacko women tryin' to take advantage of me."

"Oh, again, you have hit on the right idea but with the wrong intent. Somebody took advantage, and it was you. And now, to make matters even worse, Sana is pregnant with your child. And all I have to do to prove it is grab a swab of your nasty-ass habit off the side of your truck, run it through the DNA tests, and bang, a match is made. The only wrinkle is that Sana hasn't pressed charges, so I can't do all that. But if she changes her mind, which, as you know, women will do occasionally, she could press charges, and then we'd be on like Donkey Kong."

"Well, if she ain't pressin' charges, why you botherin' me? I could sue your Black ass for harassment."

The sheriff looked him square in the eyes.

"You don't want to go thinking things like that, Jeff, especially with your old man locked up in the state pen already serving time. We know you're running his little drug empire while he's passing the time. And we know you think he had something to do with your mom's death. Why the hell? I agree with you, though I could never prove it. You've got your head down, and you're trying to keep your nose clean until shit cools down."

Jeff felt his courage drain away like warm piss running down his pants.

"So, what the fuck we doin' here?"

The sheriff took a deep breath and waded into the stream.

"I'm gonna offer you a 'Stay out of jail card' on Sana and Tara's behalf. I want you to confess that you're the baby's father and take responsibility for the situation financially. You must provide a safe place for Sana and her baby to stay and pay child support. As we've already discussed, we'll decide your paternity, or you could marry Sana and show paternity that way. Either way, you're responsible for your actions and the fallout they caused."

Jeff looked at her like she was on fire.

"You gotta be shittin' me! Marry her! No f'ing way am I gonna do that. You must think me a complete damn fool."

"Jeff, I must commend you on your ability to call a situation for what it is and still be unable to see it clearly. As you say, I would think you a complete fool, but only if you *didn't* take this offer. Trust me when I tell you, we know what you did to Sana and her mom. We know what you're doing now with your father's drugs. So, it's only a matter of time before your arrogance catches up with you, and you end up right beside your dad in the pen. And we both know how much you'd love that. I'd give you 24 hours before one or both of you are dead on the inside."

At that moment, the group foreman stuck his head out the door and gave Jeff a "Get the fuck back in here!" look.

"I got to get goin'. Let me think on it, and we can talk again," Jeff said.

"Okay, I'll be back in 24 hours to see how your thinking is progressing. After that, I'll have to do some thinking of my own, you understand?" the sheriff asked.

Jeff stormed away as the sheriff headed back to her car.

As she started the car, she heard the whistle blow for a shift change.

Well, we're in the shit now.

CHAPTER 6

It was near closing time in the bar as "Gimme Three Steps" blasted out of the jukebox. The pool sharks had finished their game and counted their money on the seedy felt tabletops. A thick blue cloud hung over the room. The trailer park floozies worked the barstools for all they were worth. The bartender noticed Jeff had ramped up his one-sided conversation with himself. He had seen this behavior before and knew it was just a prelude to him throwing Jeff out onto the street.

"Why the fuck did she have to run out of gas there? Why didn't she check the stupid fuckin' thing before she left home? What a stupid bitch!" Jeff yelled.

"Jeff, my man, I think it's time you settled your tab and moved along. You seem to be getting a little agitated about something, and I don't need any ruckus out of you tonight. Understand?" the bartender asked, standing across from Jeff.

Jeff's head slowly rocked back like it was on a swivel, and squinting his eyes, he gave the bartender a long, hard look.

"What the hell you mean, ruckus? I ain't no goddamn ruckus. She's the goddamn ruckus!"

Then, standing up a little too quickly, he tumbled backward onto the floor. He tried his best to stand again, but gravity and a belly full of beer had other plans as he stumbled and fell about the bar, knocking over tables and chairs.

The bartender quickly rounded the counter, grabbed him by his collar, dragged him kicking and screaming to the door, and shoved him hard into the side of his truck.

"I suggest you crawl your worthless carcass into that fucking rolling nightmare of yours and sleep it off! Whatever the fuck you do, don't come back in here tonight, or it'll be real trouble."

Heeding the bartender's good advice, Jeff eventually staggered to his feet and climbed up in his truck.

"That stupid fuckin' bitch! This is all her goddamn fault. And now that fuckin' Black sheriff wants me to own my responsibility to this bitch. I'll show them how I'll own it."

Rubbing his head where it had smacked into the truck door, he drove away from the bar, weaving all over the road, continuing his rant as he headed down the highway.

"Well, if I have to marry this bitch... take care of my 'obligations' as that bitch Sheriff says... might as well get some fuckin' good out of it. Ha, fuckin' good! No, good fuckin' out of it! Yeah, yeah, yeah, that's what I should be gettin'. Some good fuckin.' Yeah!" He banged his hands on the steering wheel as if that made the statement even more emphatic.

As if karma were watching out for him, or perhaps some other divine explanation, a giant deer ran out of the woods across the road in front of his truck, and when he over-corrected, trying to miss it, he slammed into a shallow ditch. This cosmic intervention left him very rattled and badly battered, but it kept him from perhaps even more significant harm had he reached his intended destination.

An hour later, he safely made it home with a hundred bucks of his hard-earned money now in the tow truck driver's pocket. The following day, he wondered what had happened to his truck, as he had no recall of events after being thrown out of the bar.

He thought about the conversation with the sheriff and tried to summon a path forward that would catch them all by surprise, using all his cunning and skills as a world-class delinquent.

What if he did what they thought was right, apologized to them, tried to make amends, and married her? If she was his wife, hell, he could do with her whatever he wanted, as that was what his deadbeat father had always done with his mom. He might have to fake his repentance for a while and trick the bitch into thinking he'd turned over a new leaf, so he could start living with her. But he'd done far worse in the past to maintain some other brilliant plan he developed, so why should this be any different? The one thing he knew for sure was that he could not afford to support them and keep himself afloat at the same time. His shitty job at the steel mill barely kept him alive, so like it or not, if he wanted to stay out of trouble, he'd have to make this deal work with Sana.

Of course, only someone with the Darwinian survival instincts of a feral possum could ever conceive that such a deception would work, which is precisely why Jeff felt so confident.

CHAPTER 7

True to her word, the sheriff called on Jeff again the next day at the steel mill to see how his decision-making was going. She hoped he would see the light and agree to her plan, but deep down, she knew that was a long shot. And even if he did go along, she still had to get Sana and her mom on board.

The foreman saw her approach the team line again and held up his hand for her to wait right there, then yelled, "Jeff, your visitor is back again. Make whatever business you got with her quick, or it's your ass."

Jeff quietly followed the sheriff outside, wanting to make as good an impression as possible.

He shoved a plug of chewing tobacco in his mouth and shuffled his feet momentarily, trying to gather his courage.

"Well, I been thinkin' a lot about the situation with Sana and her mom and your offer, and don't shit yourself when I tell you this, okay, but I'm in. We'll need to talk about livin' arrangements and whatnot, but I'm willin' to own my mistake and try to make shit right with Sana."

The sheriff looked at him coldly as she adjusted her heavy belt.

"First, let me commend whoever this new person is standing before me on that incredible piece of acting. If I were a fool, I might buy what you're selling, but we both know bullshit when we smell it, Jeff, and boy, you stinkin' to high heaven. Second, there ain't gonna be no talk about 'living arrangements and whatnot,' so you can stop worrying about that right now. We can discuss visitation rights after the child is born, but that's all you'll get unless Sana says otherwise, which I truly don't ever see happening."

Jeff was visibly shaking now but somehow managed to keep his head from exploding.

"What the fuck then? You told me to think about it, and I did! And now you tellin' me I'm actin' the fool and can't live with the bitch even if I marry her. What the hell kinda of deal is that?"

"Well, I'll tell you, boy. It's the kind of deal that keeps your ass out of jail, at least for a little while longer. Ain't none of this about accommodating you, no sir! This deal is all about making things better for Sana and Tara. You have no choice other than to agree to and live up to your end of the bargain. If that doesn't sound acceptable to you, we'll have to discuss different plans, so what's it gonna be, Jeff?"

By now, Jeff stood defeated in all but one regard: his unbelievable stupidity. He shoved his hands down in his pants to keep from taking a swing at her. Then, pointing his finger at her, he shifted tactics.

"I'm callin' bullshit on this right now! You want me to agree to this shit, so it looks like you pullin' a fast one on a white man just goin' 'bout his business. I see you! Yeah, I see you! You don't give a shit 'bout that girl any more than I do. I ain't gonna be part of your re-election campaign. No fuckin' Mam!"

If he had left everything at that, Jeff might have gotten away with some semblance of personal victory, however ill-gotten it may have been. But his reptilian brain kicked in, and instead, he spat a giant wad of chewing tobacco on the sheriff's shoes as his closing argument.

Looking down calmly, she reached into her back pocket, pulled out a white handkerchief, and stooped to wipe her shoes clean.

Jeff watched her like a rattlesnake, coiled and ready to strike.

When satisfied with her work, she calmly resumed standing.

"Jeff, listen to me real good now. You better watch yourself damn close because, from this moment forward, I got my eye on you like a proverbial hawk. That's not a threat, boy, just a stone-cold fact. I'll be seeing you."

And with that, the sheriff adjusted her hip holster, turned, and slowly walked away. Jeff watched her leave, feeling very unsure about his next move. Then, the foreman yelled at him from the factory door, bringing him back to reality.

The shift change whistle blew in the distance.

As Jeff approached the team line, the foreman said, "I've seen you do a lot of stupid shit in my limited time with you, but that's got to be one of the dumbest things ever. I don't know what kinda shit you're mixed up in, but I'll tell you this much: that woman will have your balls on a stick before it's all over with."

Always trying to appear more confident than he was, he replied weakly, "Oh yeah, well, she best watch her step, too. That shit flows both ways."

"Get the fuck back on the line, you stupid ball-bag," the foreman said as he whacked him upside the head.

CHAPTER 8

It was late afternoon when the sheriff drove to Sana's trailer to share an update on her talks with Jeff, a conversation she did not look forward to.

If possible, the situation around the trailer looked even more pathetic than the last visit.

Sana greeted the sheriff at the door and said, "Hey, Sheriff. Come inside and tell us what you got."

She settled into the chair opposite Sana and Tara, took a deep breath, and began.

"Well, I've contacted Jeff several times, and I'll have to say that boy is even dumber than I thought. Anyway, here's what I have. At first, he said he would do the right thing, marry you, and own his mistake. But he wants to live with you, and I told him straight up that was a non-starter. Some other unpleasantness followed, as you might imagine, but that's the short story of where we left it. I wish I had better news to report."

Tara replied with a sinister chuckle. "Yeah, I bet there was some other unpleasantness. That fool thinks he's better than you for no reason other than he white and you Black. Forget that badge on your shirt. Crackers like him don' care 'bout any of that shit. They think they invincible!"

"Sana are you sure you don't want to press charges?" the sheriff asked. "We could make his life miserable and maybe shock some sense into that concrete block of his head."

"What if I met with him here and we just talked? Maybe he'd come around if he saw me as a person instead of some big threat. Besides, chargin' him makes our lives pretty miserable, too. And in case you haven't noticed, we got plenty of that as it is," Sana said quietly.

"If you decide to do that, I'd want to be here if he decides to try something dumb. Maybe the better play is to bring him in and speak to him at the jail. That would undoubtedly focus his mind and let him know we aren't messing around," the sheriff replied.

Sana knew that was a bad idea but found herself nodding in agreement anyway as another plan evolved. All she had to do was get a note to Jeff saying she'd meet with him privately, and the two of them could talk about everything. They certainly weren't making any progress trying things the sheriff's way.

When a person is exposed to domestic violence early and often, what passes for normal and acceptable behavior is anything but. Such was the case with Sana. She had seen her mom get battered and bruised countless times. She repeated the same mistakes and suffered a kind of insanity where she expected a different outcome. Sana had experienced a brutal rape, but in her mind, it was simply a big misunderstanding. If she could convince Jeff that she wasn't a severe problem, that she didn't want to be a hassle for him to deal with, maybe he would come around, and who knows, they could have some semblance of a relationship.

If Sana had only recalled the children's fable about "The Frog and the Scorpion," she could have seen where her thinking was flawed.

In the parable, a scorpion wants to cross a river but cannot swim, so it asks a frog to carry it across. The frog hesitates, afraid that the scorpion might sting it, but the scorpion promises not to, pointing out that it would drown if it killed the frog in the middle of the river. The frog considers this argument momentarily and, finding it sensible, agrees to transport the scorpion. Midway across the river, the scorpion stings the frog anyway, dooming both. The dying frog asks the scorpion why it stung him despite knowing the consequence, to which the scorpion replies, "I am sorry, but I couldn't resist the urge. It's in my nature."

"It's in my nature." These four words would soon trigger events that anyone could have foreseen.

COME
IF YOU
DARE

CHAPTER 9

It was the middle of the night as Jeff stomped around in his trailer, still stewing about his last meeting with the sheriff. His only compatriot was a dusty Big Mouth Billy Bass hanging on the wall. It couldn't respond to Jeff's tirade with its signature humor. Dead battery.

"That bitch is tryin' to ruin my life. It's high fuckin' time I stopped playin' nice and took matters into my own hands."

Billy Bass looked on in silence.

With that, he grabbed his keys and bolted out the door.

As he rolled down the highway, retracing his path to Sana's trailer, he played in his mind exactly how all this would go down.

He'd knock politely on the door, pretending all he wanted to do was talk. Then, when they let him in, as he knew they would, he'd end this whole mess once and for all.

Unfortunately for Jeff, this was not the first time Sana and Tara had experienced such a late-night intrusion from some drunk John wanting to collect his pound of flesh. So, when the big diesel rumbled into the front yard, they almost experienced a sense of relief.

"'Bout time that damn boy showed up. What took him so long?" Tara calmly asked. Then, looking over at Sana, she asked, "You ready?"

Sana nodded yes, even though she was terrified.

Jeff pulled away from the trailer into the yard, exited the still-running truck, stormed across the weedy yard, kicking bottles and cans out of his way as he went, and pounded on the front door, rattling the slatted glass.

"Bitches, I know you're in there," Jeff yelled. "I just wanna talk and see if there's a way we can avoid a whole lot of pain. Open the damned door."

Sana cautiously approached the door and spoke through the glass.

"We can talk jus' fine through this locked door. So, how you see us avoidin' all this pain you caused? You got some big idea?"

Jeff stepped back, highly annoyed. He thought for a second and then, bringing his big steel-toed work boots into action, kicked the door open. Sana took the brunt of the blow on the other side and was knocked on her back. She quickly regained her footing as Jeff stormed into the trailer. Cautiously, he stopped short just as he cleared the door. Across the room, Tara was holding a shotgun, itching for him to make another move.

"Aha, didn't see that comin', did you? Now step yo' cracker ass back outside real slow like, and we'll carry on from there," she said.

Jeff was never one to back down from a fight, even when he should. He forged ahead and played his bluff for all it was worth. This action would soon earn him nothing less than an honorary Darwin award.

"Naw, naw, you ain't gonna shoot me. You're just a scared old Black hag. You ain't gonna do nothin' at all 'cause you know if you do, it'll be the last damned thing you ever do."

Even as he tried to make his weak bluff work, he slowly inched towards the door, but not before he reached out, grabbed Sana by the arm, and quickly dragged her outside.

They stumbled outside, stumbling and falling down the front steps. Jeff quickly regained his footing, wrapped his arms around Sana's neck, and put her in a deadly choke hold.

Tara screamed out the door after Sana and quickly moved to see the scene outside. She saw no way to get a clean shot off as Jeff slowly stepped back towards his truck.

Sana was eerily calm. She thought if she didn't struggle, maybe he'd let her go or, at a minimum, not choke her as severely.

"Now, settle your crazy asses down! I just wanna talk about this deal the sheriff is tryin' to get me to take. That's all I swear!" Jeff yelled at Tara as he backtracked towards his truck.

Suddenly, Sana heard something rattling behind her as they backed across the yard towards the truck. She couldn't tell if it was Jeff's truck, which he'd left running, or something else. It wasn't long before she got her answer when a rattlesnake struck Jeff on the back of his leg, right through his heavy work pants.

"God damn, what the fuck was that?!" Jeff screamed as he let Sana go and reached for his now-aching leg.

Sana broke free and raced back towards the trailer.

Jeff kicked the snake away and started to pursue her again.

Then a shotgun blast roared past Sana's ears, just missing her head, hitting Jeff squarely in the chest and sending him flying.

Time didn't exactly stand still, but it slowed way down. Even the lightning-bug flashes seemed to take an eternity to blink out. Sana's steps to escape Jeff felt like running in heavy water. She insisted that her feet move, but they lacked any sense of urgency.

Tara stepped out of the trailer into the yard, putting a second shot into Jeff and then one into the rattlesnake for good measure.

Then Tara heard Sana's screaming as it cut through the ringing in her ears. She ripped the gun from Tara's hands, unloaded every last shell into Jeff's now barely recognizable form, and continued pulling the trigger after it was empty. Noticing she had no more shots left, her screaming intensified.

Greatly alarmed, Tara slowly backed away, giving Sana room to scream herself out.

Soon, the only sound they heard was the diesel rumble of the truck.

Both were in a state of shock and wondered precisely how in the hell things had gotten so sideways so fast.

"I knew that cracker was gonna try somethin' like this! I jus' knew it! That bullshit about doin' the right thing and ownin' his responsibility is nothin' but crazy talk. He owns that shit now! You can bet your ass on that!" Tara yelled. Then, as she walked around anxiously surveying the wreckage, she started laughing uncontrollably.

"Momma, we got to figure out what we were gonna do now. We got to get rid of him somehow. Then we got to get ourselves disappeared, 'cause when people start lookin' for him, they gonna to start lookin' for us, too. And when they see this trailer, all busted up and blood all over the damned place, we're gonna be in some deep shit," Sana said.

"I know, baby, I know. Jus' give me a sec' to think. Lord, have mercy," Tara said. Then, reacting more clearly, "Check his pockets for keys. We'll load his ass up in that truck and dump him down the road at that nasty-ass pig farm. Them Durocs will make a meal out of him by sun-up. Then, we'll get away from here as quick as possible. Now, go pack only yo' necessaries, baby, 'cause we gotta fly away from here."

CHAPTER 10

Sana and Tara cruised down the highway in Jeff's truck in the dead of night. There wasn't another soul on the road beside them, something they were genuinely thankful for.

Their world seemed small, occupying only the two-lane road and a halo of trees lit by the headlight beams. It felt like they were boring a tunnel through the darkness, heading towards the light.

Sana recalled the scene at Jeff's disposal in the sty.

The smell was almost overpowering. Everything assaulted their senses, from the funky smell to the high-pitched squeals. Luckily, Jeff's truck was so tall that they could roll him out the back over the fence. Getting him in the truck had been challenging, but getting him out was a piece of cake.

His bloodied body had no sooner hit the ground in the pigsty when the pigs descended on him in a feeding frenzy. They ripped him apart in no time, and several pigs defended their take with their immense jowls chomping away. The grunts and squeals the pigs made were frightening, and Sana was happy not to be in there where Jeff was.

What to do about leaving the trailer and their car had taken a bit more thought. Ultimately, they decided the best plan was to put things back in order as best they could and disappear. The sheriff would no doubt come calling again, but by then, with any luck other than bad, they would be well away from Jeff and his recent troubles.

"Well, gettin' rid of Jeff was as easy as you said. How'd you know them pigs would eat him up like that?" Sana asked.

Tara took a moment and stared out the window.

"When I was a little girl, I saw what pigs could do up close. We lived next to a hog farm out in the country 'cause that's the only place we could afford, and Daddy worked there, feedin' the pigs and generally lookin' after stuff. One day, a mangy old stray dog got into the pen, thinkin' he might take one of them little ones for a snack. Well, Mama Sow, she had another plan for his ass, and when he made his move, she and some of the other pigs swarmed him. Next thing you know, he's bein' made into crazy bacon. They tore his ass apart and consumed every sign of his worthless carcass. He didn't stand a chance," Tara replied.

Sana shivered at the story.

As she reflected on how close she and her mom had come to being killed by Jeff, she felt a long-dormant survival instinct trying to reactivate. Jeff's pulling her out of the trailer, combined with the nearness of the shotgun blast her mom let fly, broke something loose in her psyche, and Sana now looked at things with newfound clarity. It was as if all the years of witnessing and experiencing personal abuse had broken through a wall, and now that she had crossed that threshold, she swore to herself that things would be different. She didn't share this new perspective, but Tara would soon see a profound change.

"We got to get rid of this truck as soon as possible. It's a direct tie-back to Jeff, and besides, it looks more than a little crazy to see two Black women cruisin' aroun' in this rollin' hate machine. We need to find somewhere to stop and regroup," Sana said.

Tara looked at her with a newfound respect and a strange motherly pride. Her baby girl was changing right before her eyes. She couldn't tell how, but she damn sure knew why.

"You right, baby, we got to do all that and then some. But we got to be very careful 'bout what we say to people. They get word we on the run from killin' somebody, we'll be in a whole other world of hurt. Let's hit the next Quick Stop and see if we can find the nearest church. Them Christians is always lookin' for a good cause, and we might be jus' what they need to feel good about themselves. 'Look at me! Look at me helpin' these poor Black ladies out! Where's my halo?'"

After this, she cackled, like Sana hadn't heard for a while.

"I'm glad you feel like laughin' 'bout all this, but I'm not feelin' the funny right now."

Tara settled back down from her laughing and got very serious.

"No, you right. This shit ain't no laughin' matter, but it ain't our damn fault either! But none of that shit matters now, so we might as well find joy when we can, even if it seems crazy."

A Quick Stop store soon came into view. They exited the highway and pulled over to the side of the store, out of sight from the counter inside. They were afraid to shut the big diesel off, as it had not stopped running since the unpleasant business with Jeff.

"Here goes nothin'," and Sana switched the engine off.

They stepped out into the early morning light and stretched their bodies. They both felt strangely refreshed. It was as if being inside Jeff's truck had wrapped them in hate, stifling their will to survive.

They entered the store casually and looked for something to eat and drink. They grabbed a few packs of beef jerky and bottled drinks and made their way to the front of the store.

Sana asked the attendant behind the counter, "Hey! Can you tell us where we can find the nearest church? We're on our way to a family funeral, and our money is runnin' a little tight, and we wondered if there might be a helpin' hand."

The attendant could not have been less interested in their plight if he tried, as he offered directions to the nearest church, which he said ran a soup kitchen.

"Thank you! You have a bless'd day," Tara said, bringing her hands together in her most sincere blessing.

Back outside at the truck again, Sana's concern over starting the engine renewed. She slowly reached up and pushed the red "Start Engine" button, and much to her relief, the big diesel roared to life.

"Thank you, God! Thank you!" she said, looking up.

The Baptist Church was only a few miles away and seemed to be doing quite the charity work with the soup kitchen as patrons lined up down the street on the sidewalk. They felt this situation offered good cover, as they would be just one of the many faces seeking help.

As they drove by and pulled into the church parking lot, a few heads turned to check them out but quickly returned to their own situation. The site of this big truck with the black flag flying in the back was reason enough to look away, and the fact that two Black women were driving it seemed insane.

"Remember child, say as little as you can and don' give shit away. We jus' like all the others here, jus' a mother and daughter down on their luck, lookin' for a helpin' hand. That's all they need to know," Tara said before getting out of the truck.

"Got it. Let's go, I'm starvin'."

They crossed the street and entered the line for the meal.

No one spoke to them or even seemed to acknowledge them, which was a blessing they had hoped to receive.

Slowly, the line moved inside, and they could see the church hall packed with people of every description. The air was filled with a sense of shame and humility, tinged with extreme gratitude.

They noticed the lady who must be in charge as they moved along the serving line. She was the last of the servers and spoke kindly to everyone who passed. Her words seemed genuinely heartfelt and considerate.

"Hello, ladies. Welcome. I'm Anne. Let me know if there's anything I can do for you. I hope you have a good day."

"Thank you, Anne, for your kindness and this wonderful meal. We appreciate the helpin' hand," Sana replied.

Anne nodded respectfully, and they moved along. She moved about the dining room, checking on all her guests.

Sana and Tara felt a sense of righteousness in this woman. She seemed like someone they could trust, so when she stopped by their table, Sana asked, "Anne, our money is a little tight. Is there a shelter or a cheap hotel where we might spend a night safely?"

"We have some beds here at the church, but as you can see, the demand for help is quite high. We can always accommodate more if you don't mind being packed in a little. I wish I had better news for you."

Tara replied, "Anne, you are a blessin', and I mean that sincerely. Your kindness is much appreciated. What time should we be back for the night? I assume we can't just hang out here for the rest of the day."

Anne looked at the two of them and sensed there was more to these women than they were letting on.

"We always need helping hands in the kitchen. If you'd help us clean up and prepare the evening meal, that would be a huge help."

Sana looked for approval from her mom, and her subtle nod agreed.

"Thank you so much! We'd be more than happy to help. Jus' show us what you need," Sana said.

"You sit here and enjoy the quiet until I come back around. Things should clear out in an hour or so, and then we can get you situated."

After she left, Sana and her mom talked about their next steps.

The first order of business was to get rid of Jeff's truck. They had to devise a plausible plan to ditch the rolling nightmare and get another means of transportation. Once they broke that tie to Jeff, they could move on to other needs, like how they would start over and where this new start would occur.

Then, something caught them both by surprise.

An older couple was leaving the kitchen, and they were a mixed couple; the man was Black and the woman was white. They spoke to Anne for some time, and it was apparent they were friends or, at a minimum, regular attendees to the kitchen.

Tara told Sana, "I got an idea; tell me what you think. We'll work here today and learn what we can about Anne. She seems like someone we can trust, but we won't know until we know. If she is what I think she is, we can talk to her about dumpin' Jeff's truck."

"How does her bein' trustworthy help us with Jeff's truck?"

"We'll tell Anne we want to get rid of the truck, that it belonged to a nasty uncle-in-law who got himself all tangled up in that January 6th business. We ended up with the truck 'cause my sister couldn't stand seein' it any longer. Then I'll add some other bullshit like she should have known better than to marry that horrible white man with all his crazy MAGA ways, but what can you say? People do stupid shit all the time. She gave it to us after our old beater broke down. And now, like my sister, we're tired of attractin' the wrong kind of looks from people."

"The Sheriff was right about you. You plenty smart, even if it's in a twisted-ass, crazy way."

"We'll see just how smart I am after we talk with Anne. That story will either freak her out, and we'll move along, or she'll help us however she best sees fit," Tara said, smiling like a crocodile.

After the room cleared, Anne had time to visit with Sana and Tara. Her demeanor was very pragmatic and direct, which they both agreed was a good sign. What you saw is what you got.

"As you can see, there is a great need here in the community, and not just for serving meals. People need help with various services, from food scarcity to essential health and hygiene. I'm sure you can help with the kitchen, but is there some other more valuable service you might be able to offer? Like cleaning, doing laundry, or cutting hair?" Anne asked.

Sana perked up, "I can cut hair. I never worked in a salon or anything, but I cut and styled plenty of my friend's hair before. And my mom's hair."

"Oh, she does a great job. I could help her a little, doin' shampoos and whatnot, if that's somethin' you need," Tara added.

"I have to tell you, many of these women have been victims of abuse and domestic violence, so their outlooks are somewhat fragile. Does that sound like something you would be comfortable dealing with? If not, I'd understand, but it would be a blessing if you could help."

Tara said plainly, "I'm sorry to say that's somethin' we know little about. I won't burden you with our story just yet, but believe me when I tell you, we know what these women been through. It'd be a pleasure to help them and you out."

"Anne, you've been so kind. Thank you! So, what would you like us to do right now? We can help you here now and get to know one another better, or we can come back later," Sana asked.

"Come with me," Anne said as she stood.

They followed her inside the church and down a series of hallways and stairs until she came to a room where about ten women and their children were gathered, about 15 souls in all. Sana recognized that glazed look of despair on their faces, as she had seen it reflected in every mirror she had ever stared into.

"Ladies, I'd like you to meet Sana and her mom, Tara. Like you, they are here looking for a hand-up, so please welcome them. Also, they have volunteered to help with cutting hair and other personal beauty needs if you'd like. Again, please make them feel welcome," Anne said.

And just like that, Sana and Tara stepped into a new chapter and an unknown set of challenges.

CHAPTER 11

Anne stood and surveyed the empty shelves in the kitchen pantry. Demand for food had shot up recently and showed no signs of slowing down. She wished she could perform the miracle of the loaves and fishes from the old Bible parable, but deep down, she knew no such miracles would occur. Any such blessings would come from genuine helping hands and hearts, not prayers. Prayer might make people feel better about themselves, but whispered platitudes didn't put food on these shelves.

She turned off the lights and stepped outside into the warm air.

The first thing she noticed was Jeff's big truck, and all its hate assaulted her senses. Feeling she should be able to pick out the owner of such a rolling atrocity, she wondered who it belonged to, as no one she knew or had met recently fit that demographic. She knew there were more than a few bigots in town, but none were as bold as this character appeared to be. She heard someone call her name and turned.

"Anne! Hey! Thank so much for the meal today and the chance to help with the women. We appreciate you more than you know," Tara said, with Sana standing nearby.

"You're welcome! I hope the ladies will take advantage of your kindness and spruce themselves up a bit. Just because life beats you down doesn't mean you can't get back up and show people your best."

"We'll do what we can to make 'em feel at ease and taken care of, you know, spoil 'em a little bit," Sana said.

Tara said, "Anne, we got us a little situation that you might be able to help with." Pointing toward Jeff's truck, she continued, "See, we inherited this truck from an auntie of ours. It belonged to her no-account husband, who got himself all tangled up in that January 6th bidness a while back. Everybody told her that man was trouble, but what you gonna do? People do crazy shit, pardon me sayin' it. She got tired of all the hateful looks when she drove this big thing around town, so she passed it on to us after our old beater broke down. Now, we experiencin' them same hateful looks and would love to swap it for somethin' not quite so damned awful."

"I wondered who this thing might belong to. Folks that carry on like that are pretty easy to spot. A good friend of mine runs a little garage on the outskirts of town. Let me check with him and see if he can help you out. Do you have papers for it?"

"Yeah, you see, that's another problem. When Auntie gave it to us, she didn't have nothin' but the keys. Sorry. We hoped a mechanic or somebody could jus' part it out or somethin' like that."

"Okay, I see. I'm sure we can get something better sorted out for you. It may take a day or two."

"Oh, thank you, Anne, thank you! You are truly an angel," Sana said, hugging her.

"Bless you, Anne, bless you," Tara said, fighting back tears.

"You ladies are too kind. One day, you will return this kindness to someone else. I'm counting on that. That's what I'm investing in."

Anne wondered what was behind the truck as they went their separate ways. There was a story there, and she couldn't help but feel it was dark and dangerous. Anything she could do to put that chapter of their lives farther in the past would be worth the effort.

She snapped a few pictures of the truck to show her friend David down at his shop.

CHAPTER 12

Delores had been calling Sana, but no one was picking up.

She feared the worst might have happened with Jeff and called the sheriff to see what she felt might be the best course of action.

"Hey, Sheriff. Delores here. I've been trying to follow up with Sana and Tara on their business with Jeff, but no one is answering. I feel we should go out there and check on them. Thoughts?"

"Well, that doesn't sound good. I'll meet you out there in case we find something unexpected. Can you meet me now?"

"Yes. See you soon."

The sheriff recalled her last unpleasant encounter with Jeff as she drove to the trailer. There was no doubt in her mind that he was part of the silence they were now experiencing. The only question was how he was involved and what happened to the girls.

Knowing what she did about Tara, she could have told him he might want to think twice before tangling with her again. She is a survivor of the first order. Someone like Jeff might get the drop on her when she's passed out drunk and, in a bind, but she wouldn't let that happen twice. No sir. That gal would be ready for his ass the next time, if there were one.

As she came down the drive, she noticed Delores had already arrived and was walking around the yard.

"Hey, Sheriff, thanks for meeting me out here on such short notice. I've taken a quick look around, and the only thing that looks suspicious out here is that dead rattlesnake. It looks like someone blew it away with a shotgun or something, but I've never seen that much blood before when I've seen snakes get splattered on the road."

The sheriff took a good look then said, "Well, Delores, there's a good reason you haven't seen a snake bleed that much before because I'm pretty sure that's not snake blood. Someone, or some other thing, was shot here and moved. Let's check out the trailer and see what that looks like."

Delores knocked on the door and spoke through the slatted glass.

"Sana? Tara? You guys in there? It's Delores and the Sheriff."

No response, just the buzzing sound of the growing fly population.

"Let me go in first," the sheriff said.

She approached the door cautiously, unsure of what awaited on the other side. Would it be a booby trap of some sort waiting to blow her head off or a couple of dead bodies?

She noticed the shattered latch plate when she inched the door open. Carefully pushing it further open, she stepped inside. The room was the same as when she last saw it. No better, but thankfully, no worse.

Delores stepped into the trailer and, after taking a quick look around, said, "So, what are you thinking now, Sheriff?"

"Somebody kicked this door open, completely shattering the latch. You can see the giant boot-print on the bottom part of the door. Other than that, the place looks as depressing as ever, which, oddly enough, is a good thing. So, whatever happened here happened outside, where we see all that blood on the ground. The girls' car is still here, which is a mystery to me. I'll check on our boy Jeff and see what he says. I'll also have my lab boys come out here and get a sample of this blood, just in case."

"Okay, Sheriff. Thanks again for following up on this. It doesn't look good for someone. The only thing is, who?"

As she drove from the trailer, the sheriff flipped a mental coin about whether she should visit Jeff's house or workplace. House it was.

Arriving 15 minutes later, she could see plenty of evidence of Jeff. He had an overly large "TRUMP" flag hanging off the side of his trailer and a recycling bin overflowing with Budweiser cans. Deep ruts were visible in the grass, a makeshift driveway made by his big dually. A big dog was chained outside the front door and started barking furiously as soon as she stepped out of the car. She fully expected Jeff to stick his head out the door and yell at the dog, but otherwise, there wasn't a sound. She knocked on the door and announced herself but was greeted only with silence.

Next stop: the steel mill.

Pulling into the steel mill parking lot, she searched for Jeff's truck. She didn't see it, but the place was huge, so maybe he parked elsewhere.

As she made her way over to where they had met up with Jeff before, the line foreman saw her and was surprised by her appearance.

"Howdy, Sheriff. What brings you out today?"

"Well, I'm looking again for your man, Jeff. Is he about?"

The foreman looked surprised. "No. I thought maybe you'd locked his ass up after that stunt he pulled last time you were here. He didn't show today, but he's hardly a star employee, so we didn't worry too much."

"Well, I'll just have to look elsewhere then. Thanks for your time."

Back in the car, she felt she should call in a search for Jeff's truck, but for some reason, she decided to hold off just in case he showed up the next day or so—no need to stir things up when maybe there might be a simple explanation.

Making a similar leap with the girls wasn't as easy, but she didn't know where they might be. And since she knew of no next-of-kin, nobody would know or care that they were missing.

CHAPTER 13

David's property looked like a car graveyard when seen from above. Cars from the last half century covered several acres of land. Some had been there so long that small trees were growing from the windows. Iron apparently made an excellent fertilizer because weeds quickly covered it wherever a car sat.

Anne pulled up in front of David's shop, and his head immediately popped out from under the hood of a car he was working on. He smiled as she got out and walked over.

"Well, hello, stranger. What brings you out today?" David said as he embraced her in a bear hug.

"It's good to see you, too," Anne said, catching her breath. "I have a couple of ladies down at the church who you could use an assist, and I think you are just the person to help them out."

David looked at her with concern. He didn't know what her "ask" would be, but he hoped it didn't involve something like attending church. He loved Anne's work at the church and supported her as much as he could, but the whole church thing was not his cup of tea.

"Don't worry, this favor is something you can accommodate. These ladies inherited a big, nasty truck decked out with a black American flag in the back and are looking to rid themselves of the rolling nightmare. I took some pictures for you to check out. I thought maybe you could part it out or something. They don't have papers, and I'd prefer not to press them on the issue."

Reading between the lines, David took her phone and looked at the pictures of the truck.

"Wow, I can see why they'd want to get rid of this thing. What's that all down the side? Looks nasty. Anyway, lots of guys around have this model truck, and they're always looking for used parts, so that shouldn't be a problem."

"Well, there's one more little wrinkle. I was hoping you could swap some other vehicle for the truck. It doesn't have to be much, just reliable and something these ladies could get around in."

"Anne, there's always 'just one more little wrinkle' with you, right?" He thought momentarily and then said, "I have an old beater they might be interested in. It's a high miler, but I've taken care of it since it was new, so I know it's solid. Why don't you bring the ladies by, and we can do a deal?"

"Thank you, David. I know they will be so pleased. I'll bring them by tomorrow if that works for you," Anne said, hugging him.

"Lord willing, I'll be right here, and this damned car I'm working on won't be."

Anne felt good about helping Sana and Tara with the truck as she drove away. She hoped to settle them into their roles as local beauticians, and all would work out. Of course, she knew "working out" was always relative. At least they'd be in a more stable environment and could offer her a much-needed hand.

CHAPTER 14

The community hall in the church's basement, where the women slept, was eerily quiet. The church pews creaked and popped on the floor above them as the building cooled down. It sounded like someone was moving around in the dark when the only activity was dust motes settling on the hymnals and collection plates.

Sana and Tara were nestled in their cots in the corner and listened to the whispered conversations between the other women.

It was obvious that some of these women had been in the care of Anne and the church for quite some time. There was the telltale sign of acquired piety—that sense of meeting someone who isn't quite what they'd have you believe they are. Like when a homeless person says, "Have a blessed day," after you've turned down their request for money, casting their anger your way in the form of a contemptuous empty blessing. Their masks covered a lot, but not everything.

Tara knew a lot about people and their masks—what they concealed, but more importantly, what they inadvertently revealed.

Many of her Johns had telltale signs of being married—light tan lines on their fingers where they had just removed a wedding band. The ever-searching glances around the bar for someone who might recognize them in a strange place, and most of all, a bold eagerness for straight-up sex with no strings attached in the most unlikely of venues, be it a bathroom stall or the backseat of a car in a dark corner of the parking lot.

And these masks were not specific to any one sex—men and women alike sported them to enact fantasies held at bay.

"Well, we made it through another day. Tomorrow, we'll meet up with Anne and figure out the whole beauty shop situation. I hope she can help us with that truck," Sana said.

"That'd be a big monkey off our backs if we could dump that thing. I feel like we can trust Anne, but we gots to be 100% certain. Remember what Keb Mo sang? "Actions speak louder than words.""

Sana smiled at the thought of music and tried to go to sleep.

She thought of happier times when she and her few girlfriends would sit around and braid each other's hair, dishing dirt on what they thought of so-and-so dating this girl or that.

That was a much simpler time, the "Before" time, as she now called the period before Jeff had entered their lives. Now, they were struggling with the completely unknown "After" times.

But now, Sana was better equipped to deal with the unknown, and she would no longer put herself in harm's way if there were any way she could avoid it. The combination of dealing with Jeff and the baby growing inside her had unlocked a confidence and cunning she never knew could exist.

Then sleep took her.

But rather than the peaceful sleep she'd longed for, she was beset in a surreal apocalypse, like the body collectors of old, ringing the bell and yelling, "Bring out your dead. Bring 'em all." Only these bodies were ghost encounters from her brief, and as she'd always considered it until now, an insignificant past. These terrifying apparitions came through the walls, up from the ground, and down from the sky. Some swirled and grew, taking on the dimensions and form of an emotional tornado, piercing screams emanating and echoing from deep within, trailing off, and then circling back like a trapped dance partner in a lunatic death waltz. Other phantoms were a furious wave of pelting fists, crashing down all over her body and pounding her like a hurricane from all sides. Flashes of her mom were mixed in among the gathering storms, and Sana could see she was dealing with her nocturnal hell-scape.

Then the bottom fell out of her consciousness, and they were both infinitely small, no larger than a grain of sand. Every object in her vision was vastly more significant than her, posing a threat. One false step, and they would be crushed underneath. They were on the dark side of hell, where not even the light from Satan's eyes dared intercede.

Even as this torment enveloped her, Sana was not afraid but instead gathered untold power from it. She could sense every cell in her body growing in strength and potential for creating and controlling misery, increasing exponentially with each division.

The child she was carrying, conceived in a hateful act, was altering her body and mind in ways she could not understand. These terrifying acts of violence unleashed a dark form of malignant euphoria deep within her psyche. Generations of white supremacy, arrogance, and hatred coursed through the fetus's developing veins. And now, after Jeff's vicious attack, it ran rampant through hers as well. These racists and misogynist pigs created all the laws to keep people like her in their place—a place of subservience. But now, she was seizing that power through her unborn child, and she would unleash it on anyone who ever tried to put her down again.

Then, a bright flash and thunderous sound jolted her awake.

When she awoke and realized it was all a dream, Tara held her hands, saying everything would be alright.

"You okay, baby, you okay. You jus' had a bad nightmare is all, thrashing around and shit. You screamed out, but you safe now."

"God almighty, it was all so real! You were there with me, and all hell surrounded us. And at one point, we were so small that anythin' could have killed us, and no one would know or care."

Tara comforted her as best she could, and as was her way always, she spoke her unique truth, this time to the subject of dreams.

"Baby, dreamin' is jus' your mind tryin' to work out some shit out it can't quite crack otherwise. Sleep opens the doors that being awake keeps locked up tight. But you know better than me that dreams come true, but not in some happy bullshit way most people believe. Bad shit happens in your dreams, and then it happens in life. The trick is to take what we see in dreams, the good and the bad, and use that shit to spot trouble before it gets ahold of yo ass."

Sana settled down and sorted through the wreckage of her dream.

Once again, she was amazed at the simplicity and clarity of her mother's thinking, even though she knew Tara had no idea what had just occurred in her dreams, much less how Sana would engage this knowledge in the near future.

Sana determined they could harness great power by living on the margins, in the space considered "the margin of error" by the rest of the world. There, they were undetectable and unseen, of little concern. They were just something the rest of the world ignored. Out of sight, out of mind. That's where her true power would emanate.

CHAPTER 15

David's head popped up from under the hood of an old beater he was working on when he heard the big RAM dually roll into the drive. *Holy shit! No wonder these ladies want to get rid of that thing.*

Anne parked behind Sana and her mom and walked the ladies up to chat with David.

"Hey, David, I'd like you to meet Sana and her mom, Tara. Ladies, this is my good friend David."

"Hello, ladies. It's good to meet you. Anne tells me you want to trade this truck for something a little less attention-grabbing, and from what I can see here, I'm right there with you."

"Yes, yes, yes! When our Auntie gave it to us, we were so thankful for the ride, 'cause our old beater of a car had jus' died. But since then, all we get is mean and hateful looks. And wit' crazy like in today's world, you never know what kinda shit some people might pull, so we'd like to jus' move it on down the road," Tara said.

"Well, I've got a high-miler car that I've serviced since it was new that could work for you. It's a little rough on the paintwork, but solid where it counts. Follow me out back, and you can check it out," David said as he led them to the rear of the garage.

Sitting in the chain-linked fence area was the perfect vehicle for them: a tan 1999 Buick Le Sabre. The paint on the center of the hood and the top was worn away from too many washes by overly loving hands. There was a long crack at the lower edge of the windshield, but otherwise, it was precisely what they were hoping for. A deep hole was worn through the carpet at the base of the gas pedal, classic evidence of a one-driver owner. You couldn't ask for a less attention-grabbing car.

"It's perfect! This car is exactly what we need. You sure you're okay doin' a straight-up swap? We don't have any extra cash, so I'm hopin' you are," Sana said.

"Yeah, I think I can make a straight swap work. Lots of guys around here drive these big rigs. Frankly, I think most of 'em are compensating for something, if you get my drift."

"Oh, David, stop it with that kind of talk," Anne said, blushing and feigning embarrassment. "And thank you so much for helping these ladies out. We all appreciate it."

"Thank you, thank you, thank you!" Sana and Tara said, catching David in a big hug.

"Wow, I didn't see that coming. Let me fetch the keys for you, and you gals can be on your way."

Sana and Tara followed Anne back to the church, talking as they drove.

"Well, baby, that's one big ass monkey off our backs. Thank God he swapped that truck for us," Tara said.

"I feel like the weight of the world jus' fell off my shoulders. Now, we can focus on our next steps. Settin' up our little salon will give us a chance to recover a bit."

Back in town again, Anne led them to their new work area.

It was an old boarded-up barber shop just around the corner from the church. Anne opened the door, and they all stepped inside. The air was stale and dank, and everything had a coating of dust and dead flies on it.

"I know it's not much to look at now, but I think we can make this work with a little effort. Luckily, the previous owners just walked away during COVID-19 and left all the fixtures here. It needs a good scrubbing, a fresh coat of paint, and some changed-out light bulbs to get it back in shape. What do you think?" Anne asked.

"Oh, Anne, this will be jus' fine, jus' fine," Tara said. "You got scissors and combs and such? We ain't got none of that kinda stuff."

"Not yet, but we can get shampoos, conditioners, and whatnot from the local Walmart. The manager over there helps us out a lot. She's a saint in my book."

Sana said, "Okay, Anne, we got this now, so you go do whatever you need to do. Next time you see this place, it will look like somethin'."

"Yes. Thank you again for all your help with the truck. That David is a angel, for sure. You, too!" Tara added.

"Oh, and thank you for what you will do for these ladies. I know they will be excited to be pampered a little. Take care."

After Anne had left and had cleared the view out the front window, Tara said, "Okay, come on, and let's whip this thing into shape. Then we can check out the rest of town and see what we got."

It took some doing, but they finally got the salon in order after a couple of hours. All they needed now were supplies from Anne, and they could get started. They even came up with a name: Heaven Sent Salon. Sana and Tara felt hiding behind their own bit of holiness was only natural. They were playing the game the same as everyone else. Nobody needed to know what had sent them their way.

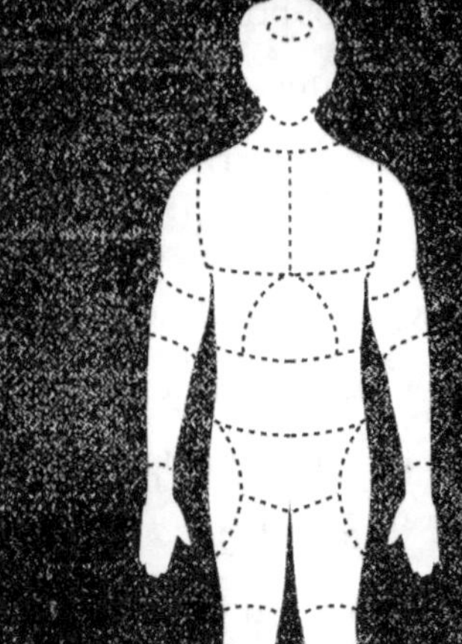

CHOICE
CUTS

CHAPTER 16

The sky was a deep cerulean blue. The air was clean and crisp. Good tunes were playing on the radio. They almost didn't have a care in the world. Almost. It was late afternoon, just before the golden hour, and Sana and Tara were cruising around town in their new ride, amazed at how invisible they were in this car. No one gave them a second look.

The dark green "Pine Scent" air freshener dangling from the rear-view mirror was a classic touch. *Remove the entire plastic wrap for a complete pine scent experience*; the label instructions were precisely the advice they needed to combat the overwhelming smell of patchouli from the previous owner. All they required to be completely invisible was to add a small gold cross on a chain hanging down from the mirror.

Like many small towns in the area, there was a church on practically every corner of the central square, but the town fell away quickly once you left the main square. Many of the shops were boarded up, and there was a general sense of depression about the whole scene. This once-thriving town had seen better days, but there was no guarantee it would ever see them again.

They rounded the corner and spotted the Walmart. Sadly, it was one of their baby stores with just the essentials and not much else, and not one of the behemoth Super Centers with anything you could want.

As they pulled into the parking lot, something caught Sana's eye.

A young white girl who looked to be 25 or so was pulling an overly large trailer behind a shiny Ford F-250 truck. The enclosed trailer had a huge vinyl wrap that advertised, MOBILE BUTCHERY - WE COME TO YOU.

As the traffic light turned green, her imagination suddenly shifted into overdrive, and she could see herself inside this trailer.

She was inside, working feverishly alongside the girl, hacking a freshly killed carcass to pieces with a saw. The girl had carefully marked lines all over the body with a fat pen so she would know exactly where to cut, just like the posters in high-end butchery shops, showing which parts of the animal were hams, shoulders, loins, and the like. Then she realized the carcass was not an animal, at least not in the traditional sense, but a man. It was gruesome work, but she was all in, hacking, sawing, and carving as if her life's purpose had finally been revealed.

Her baby, who, until now, had been just an inanimate passenger, suddenly kicked to life, twisting and moving inside her. The more she hacked away at the body, the more excited and active it became. The shared moment was exhilarating for Sana. Then, the sound of a car horn and yelling behind her jolted her out of her vision.

"Girl, what the world are you smilin' 'bout? We betta get a move on 'fore these crackers start shittin' they pants and whatnot. You want me to drive?" Tara asked.

"No, no, I got it. I jus' had a little daydream moment there, thinkin' about all the new shit we got going on."

The baby settled down again as they walked through the store.

It had been a while since either of them felt comfortable enough to go out in public, but now that the link to Jeff and the truck was broken, they were feeling better about things—far from unencumbered, but better.

As they made their way to the back of the store to the meat counter, Sana spotted the girl she had seen driving the MOBILE BUTCHERY trailer, and the baby started kicking and squirming inside her with renewed energy. The girl talked animatedly with the butcher behind the counter, telling him what items she had for sale but seemed to be having little success.

The butcher wiped his bloody hands on his apron and finally relented.

"Okay, I'll take any pork items you have, but I've got more beef and chicken than I can say grace over. Just pull around to the back of the store, and we can show you where to put it."

The girl was so excited that she practically jumped up and down. She thanked the butcher and hurried back outside to her rig.

Sana tapped her mom's shoulder and motioned for them to leave. Once outside, Sana drove around to the back of the store, where she hoped to meet the girl.

The baby was kicking wildly again, a sign that Sana was beginning to understand more clearly.

She wasn't sure exactly what she would say to this stranger, but she felt compelled by some inner power to do so. As Sana approached, the girl opened her trailer and started moving items into the store.

"Hey, I'm Sana, and this is my mom, Tara. We noticed you talkin' with the meat man inside. I never seen a mobile butchery before. What exactly do you do with this thing?" Sana asked.

Surprised by Sana's sudden appearance, the girl stopped and wiped her hands on her apron.

"Hey, Sana. It's good to meet you. I'm Jesse. Well, it's kind of like what the name here implies. Instead of you having to take your animals to the butcher to have them processed, I come to you and do it right there on your farm. Do you deal with livestock?"

"Oh no, not me! I never thought about how that whole business works. I see chicken and hamburger meat in the freezer and never wonder how it got there. Do you make a lot of money doin' that?"

"I guess that depends on what you call 'a lot'. I make enough to get by pretty well, but I could always do more. I'm always looking for work."

Then she started back at her task, speaking as she went.

"Let me know if you run into anyone who could use my service. I'll give you some cards to hand out."

"That'd be great. I'll ask Anne at the church if she knows anybody. She seems to know everybody in town. Hey, if you ever need a haircut or a trim, we're openin' a little salon across the way—Heaven Sent Salon. I'd love to learn more about what you do."

"I may just take you up on that. Working in this trailer out in the blazing sun can get kind of hot, and this long hair only makes it worse."

Jesse walked to the truck's cab, got a handful of cards, and handed them to Sana.

"Great! Thanks for these. You have a nice day."

Back in the car, Tara looked at Sana curiously.

"So, what exactly was THAT all about? You ain't never thought for a second about anythin' like what that girl is involved in."

"Well, we both doin' a lot of crazy things now that we ain't never done before, wouldn't you say? I can't say why or how right now, but that girl will help us out in a big way one day."

Tara gave her a long, hard look but remained silent, letting things play out as Sana saw fit.

Meanwhile, the baby was as active as ever. It seemed to be gaining strength and control, and Sana was more than willing to relinquish it.

CHAPTER 17

The sheriff took another ride to Jeff's trailer to see if he had reappeared. It had been a couple of weeks, and everything was quiet—unsettlingly so. The girls had not shown up, dead or alive, and as far as she could tell, neither had Jeff.

When she arrived, the only thing that greeted her was his starving guard dog still chained to the trailer. He was so weak from not being fed that he couldn't muster even a whimper. The grass was starting to cover the bottom of the trailer, so it was clear no one was around. Even the deep ruts created by his truck were starting to weed over.

The sheriff radioed the station and asked Animal Control to come out and deal with the poor dog. Next, she asked to be patched through to the magistrate to get started on a search warrant to enter the trailer.

I don't know what happened to you, Jeff, but I'm pretty sure I don't have to worry about keeping an eye out for you any longer.

And with that, she got back in the car and left.

Feeling confident now that Jeff was gone, or at least missing, she put out an APB for his truck. Hopefully, that would turn up something somewhere. And since the girl's car was still at their trailer, she had few options left to find them other than filing a "Missing Persons" report, even though she knew in her soul that would do no good. These girls were just gone. The only question that remained was under what circumstances had they disappeared.

The sheriff had one more string she could pull on: Jeff's father.

So, she headed out to the prison for a quick chat. She felt sure the father had not heard from Jeff and would be spooked by her asking after him. He wouldn't have to say a word; his body language would do all the talking.

Her suspicions were confirmed as he sat across from her.

"So, Sheriff, what the hell are you doin' out here hasslin' me? You ain't got nothin' better to do?"

"I'm checking in to see how you're getting along. Your boy Jeff has gone AWOL, so I wondered if you've heard from him lately. I do hope he's all right. I mean, who's gonna take care of your business if he's up and gone?"

She'd hit the desired nerve square on the head as the father looked at her uncomprehendingly. All the semblance of control left his face, replaced by straight-up fear. If Jeff was gone, and he firmly believed that to be the case, his goose was as good as cooked. He had visions of being shivved in the yard by any number of inmates on the take from the outside.

"I ain't seen or heard from Jeff in a while, so can't help you there, Sheriff. I reckon you'll have to do some actual police work for a change, tryin' to find him rather than comin' 'round here and hasslin' me. I hate that for you."

"Why thank you for that sentiment, kind sir? I appreciate you. I'll keep you in the loop on Jeff, but in the meantime, take care. I'd hate to learn of some mishap taking place, so you have a good day now."

Back in his cell, his mind was collapsing. Everything he saw now took on a sinister dimension, from quick glances to long stares to maniacal laughter and banging on the bars. How long would it be before outside forces called him to task? A day, a week, a month? Then, as he stepped through the door to his cell, all was made clear. He felt the first few quick jabs of the shiv under his ribs before collapsing, and then everything went black.

CHAPTER 18

Anne looked out over the crowd in the dining hall, struck by the seemingly endless need displayed there. Strange faces turned into familiar ones over time, and there was a somewhat predictable turnover, but the demand never subsided or showed any signs of diminishing. It simply changed, like the seasons.

At that moment, Sana and Tara entered the hall and gave her a friendly wave. Anne waved back.

"Hello, ladies. How are you today?"

"We good, we good! I hope you are doin' okay," Tara said.

"I was just thinking about how well you two seem to be making out at the salon. I could not be prouder of you. I hope you feel the same."

"Oh, thank you, Anne, thank you! Yes, we're blessed to have the shop to go to. It took us a little bit to get settled, you know, and for the women to feel okay 'round us, but hey, that's just how it is. They don't know us, and we don't know them. That old song. People's afraid of change, even somethin' like a new hairdo," Sana said.

"We need to get you in and let us spoil you for a little bit. You work so hard here all the time. It'd be good for you to let someone else fuss over you for a while," Tara said.

"I do need to get over there. I'll check my calendar and see when I can pop over. You two have a great day."

As the ladies walked away, both felt good about what Anne had said. Their plan to reestablish themselves in a new community was working, and the past seemed to have given up trying to track them down. But none of that meant they could drop their guard. If anything, they needed to redouble their efforts at moving on. Sana was getting larger by the day, and the baby was enforcing its will more than ever.

One day, out of the blue, Jesse popped into the salon. Sana was very excited to see her.

"Hey, Jesse! How are you?"

"I'm doing okay. Work is slow, so I thought it might be a good time to drop in and see you guys. It looks like you're doing pretty well. I hope that's the case."

"Yes, yes! We've managed to make our way okay."

"Have a seat over here, and let's get you all spruced up. What are you thinkin' about for this new look?"

"Well, like I said when we first met, working in my trailer gets really hot, and pulling it up in a pony only helps so much. So, I'm thinking of something short and cool."

"Short and sweet it is! Lay back here, and let's get you shampooed."

As Sana went about cutting her hair, Jesse started talking about her life and some of the troubles she'd encountered. She had married young, right out of high school, and that's when her problems began. They moved away to a place where she didn't know anybody. Her husband, who had been a jock on the football team, turned out to be a world-class deadbeat. He only wanted to sit around in their small apartment and smoke weed; working and making a living was the last thing on his mind. And to make things worse, he forbade her to get a job. One thing leads to another; the next thing she knows, he's beating her daily. But as bad as it was, it took her a long time to realize she needed to leave. She had become entirely dependent on him, even though he provided next to nothing in return. So, when he went to search for his weekly weed stash, she packed a few belongings in an old backpack, bolted, and never looked back.

"Damn! That sounds awful. Where is he now?" Sana asked.

"Honestly, I have no idea. When I ran away, I got help from a group working with battered women in town. They helped me deal with my mental state and get a restraining order in place against my husband. They even put me in touch with some job opportunities. That's how I got into butchery. My first job was working at a grocery store, helping behind the meat counter. At first, I was sickened by the thought of dealing with all that blood and stuff, but then something changed. I saw that job as a chance to do something with my life on my terms, and I would make it work."

"I'm sorry, Jesse, I need to step away for just a sec," Sana said, stepping back in distress. "This baby is kickin' my bladder like it's a damn soccer ball or somethin'. I'll be right back."

Tara followed her into the bathroom to check on her.

"You all right, child? You lookin' kinda peeked."

"Yeah, I'll be alright, I think. The baby just got overly excited listenin' to Jesse's story. I'm ain't sure what that's all about, but I'll tell you one thing: it gets your attention."

After a few minutes, Sana returned to the chair and looked at Jesse in the mirror.

"You okay? I hope I didn't upset you too bad with my bucket of woe," Jesse said.

"Oh no, nothin' like that. I'm sure I could shock you with what's in my bucket, so don't worry."

"So, tell me how you ended up here cutting hair."

Tara shot Sana a hot look that said, *Be damn careful, girl.*

Sana nodded, *Message received* to Tara.

"Well, that's a much longer tale than I can get into right now. But I tell you what, meet me after closin', and we'll swap more bucket tales." They both laughed at that.

"Okay."

Sana focused on finishing her work and finally asked Jesse what she thought, showing her the back of her head in the mirror.

"It looks really great! And I can already tell it's going to be a lot cooler. Thank you!"

"Perfect then. So, I'll see you later, and we can chat more."

After she left, Tara started up.

"Child! What you think you doin'? You can't be tellin' that girl nothin' 'bout your past. You gots to keep that shit locked down tight."

"I know, Mama, I know. I got no intention of tellin' her my past, at least not all of it. But if I share with her that we were both battered and abused by some evil fuck; that might make a strong connection."

She didn't detail what exactly she would share with Jesse, but Tara knew better than to pry too much. Do that, and doors close.

"Jus' be careful, baby. You want me to come along?"

"No, I think it's best if it's just the two of us for now."

Even as she said this, she knew three souls would be engaged in conversation: Sana, Jesse, and her unborn baby. And as she realized now, the baby was forcing the issue more than she was.

CHAPTER 19

Since meeting Jesse, Sana's dreams had taken on a particular theme, or rather, like the lenticular process in photography, minor variations on a specific theme, where each vision is similar but different enough to count as a singular event.

They always start the same way. Sana finds herself inside Jesse's trailer, and they are both working feverishly on a freshly killed corpse. The tools she has at her disposal are very familiar, even though she has never done anything remotely like this. The bodies they cut apart are also of a theme, but very different. Some are very young, others are older. But all have one unifying quality: they are all domestic violence practitioners. Most are men, but occasionally, a woman will be on the table.

After carefully marking and cutting the bodies into their separate parts—head, cheeks, hocks, shoulders, loins, ribs, and hams—they process and package them for sale. They trim the ribs to standard items—short ribs, spareribs, whole ribs, and half racks. They grind organs and other bits of offal and make sweetbreads or sausages, a favorite among specific clientele. Only in dreams could it be this way. Or is it?

As Sana walks down the street to meet Jesse, she maintains all this nocturnal knowledge of her butchery operations. She can't help but wonder how close her dreams are to reality, and she hopes this thought will drive the conversations forward.

Jesse sees her enter the cafe and yells.

"Hey, Sana, over here."

Sana heads over and plops into the booth.

"Hey, Jesse. I been by this place dozens of times but never stopped in. I like it. What are you havin'?"

"Just a Coke for me. You?"

"I'll do the same."

The waitress walked over and took their order.

Sana weighed into the void first.

"That was some tale you told at the shop today. I'm sorry you had to go through all that. At least it was only you who had to leave, and you didn't have a baby to deal with."

Jesse dropped her head.

"Yeah, about that. I didn't tell you the worst of it. Shortly after we got married, I did get pregnant by accident. We hadn't planned on it, not for a second, but unexpected shit happens when you're scrumpin' like rabbits and not being safe. Anyway, Bart, that's my ex. He lost his shit when I told him he was about to be a dad, and he started beating and kicking me like a wild man. I had two fractured ribs and a bunch of other cuts and scrapes that got covered up with a ridiculous story: she fell out of the attic trying to get some Christmas lights down. But the worst part is that I lost the baby. And not just that, he beat me so badly that I lost the chance ever to have a baby again, even if I wanted one."

Sana looked at her with newfound respect and admiration.

"Damn, Jesse, that's terrible. I'm sorry to hear all that."

Choosing her moment carefully, Sana continued.

"Well, like I said, I know a little about that kind of life. My mom strayed off the path in middle school, havin' sex with boys for money, cuttin' class, and fuckin' up every which way. And just like you, the next thing she knows, I'm part of her life. I got no idea who my dad is. He could be any number of people, from pimps to Johns. When I was growin' up, there was always a stream of strangers comin' and goin', some leavin' my mom a bloody mess. But if that's all you've ever known, you think it's normal. You don't ask questions, you don't fight back; you just take the shit and hope you survive it until the next time comes along."

Jesse shook her head.

"It looks like things are better for you guys now. I know my life is better, and I'll never let myself be put in that situation again. Never."

Sana changed topics.

"Tell me 'bout the mobile butchery business. Better yet, can we check out your trailer? I'd love to see what all you got in there."

Jess pauses and says, "I did not see that coming. Sure, let's finish our drinks and check we'll check it out."

Walking down the street, they chatted about this and that, avoiding their past traumas like strangers on an unfamiliar road. Sana's baby, however, was uniquely energized by what they were about to see. It knew what was in store and wanted to feel its hard reality, even if only through its mother's touch. Sana could feel its excitement growing along with her own.

Jesse pulled out her keys, unlocked the big padlock, swung the latch down, and opened the trailer.

"Well, here it is, my little enterprise. It's not much to look at, but it gets the job done."

Sana took a moment, then stepped inside. She felt instantly and utterly familiar with everything. She recognized the electric saws, the long-bladed carving knives, Jesse's favorite six-inch boner, the big-bladed cleavers, and the meat grinder. The small refrigerator where Jesse stored collagen casings for all kinds of sausage. The brown kraft paper and twine used for wrapping various cuts of meat. She could close her eyes and select any tool or object Jesse might ask for.

But when she reached up and touched the large grappling hook in the middle of the trailer, used for suspending carcasses while she worked, her baby went wild, kicking and squirming. It was like an electric shock had entered her system. The moment she withdrew her hand, the baby settled down again.

"This feels so familiar. Like I been here many times, workin' alongside you. I know that's ain't so, but it feels like we've made a real connection workin' in here before today. How can that be?"

Jesse looked confused.

"I'm not sure how that could be since I know that until just a few minutes ago, no one has ever set foot in here, not even paying clients. I like my privacy when I work. That's a hard and fast rule."

Sana said, "I ain't the only one who feels a strong connection. My baby's been goin' crazy since I asked about seein' inside here. It's like it's been here before and remembers. Put your hands on my baby."

Sana grabbed Jesse's hands and gently put them on both sides of her visibly moving belly.

Then, as Jesse's hands touched Sana's belly, something essential and carnal fluttered deep inside her body. Her eyes dilated entirely, leaving just black holes burning into her skull. It felt like a long-lost connection was trying to be re-established, but the distance was too great for the energy to cross. She closed her eyes to focus on what was happening, and as she did so, dark visions of Sana's past swirled across Jesse's mind.

She was there the night Jeff appeared at the trailer with Sana and Tara. She felt the door knock her down as Jeff kicked it in. He grabbed her and pulled her outside. She heard and felt the shotgun blast from Tara. Finally, she imagined it was her, not Sana, pulling the trigger and unloading everything into her ex-husband's body, not Jeff.

The fluttering sensation she had felt deep inside just seconds before was now fully locked in, and a sinister, depraved energy flowed freely from Sana's baby to Jesse. She slowly took her hands away and stepped back to look Sana in the eyes. Her eyes were once again their hazel brown color.

"I was there, with you and your mom, the night someone broke in and tried to kill you. I saw it happen. He grabbed you and pulled you outside. It was terrifying. Not only was I there, but I took part in it; I shot my ex-husband dead. How can that be?" Jesse asked, grasping at comprehension.

Sana took her hands in hers and tried to calm her down.

"I'm sorry you saw that. I didn't know that would happen. Honest to God, I didn't know. Are you okay?"

"Yes, I think so. It was just so real. The crazy thing is, I wasn't scared or anything. Instead, I was pissed, like really pissed. All that shit I went through with my husband flashed back through me in the form of relentless rage."

Sana looked at her for a long while, gauging whether to unload what she was thinking. Fuck it, here goes.

"Well, as bad as that was, that wasn't the worst. This little demon seed you feel movin' inside me is Jeff's, the guy you saw in the vision. A few months before that happened, he raped me and my mom one night in that trailer after pretendin' to be all helpful and offerin' us a ride home when our car ran out of gas. I'll spare you all the other shit that went down with that scumbag, but trust me when I tell you, he had it comin'."

"Oh, Sana, I'm so sorry that happened to you and your mom. Your secret is safe with me."

Then, thinking back to Sana's earlier comments about her trailer being very familiar, she asked, "So, have you been in here before? I mean, in a vision, like I was in your trailer? I don't see how that could be, but then again, how the fuck could I just have imagined what I saw?"

Sana turned and calmly ran her hands over the worktop.

"Yes, many times. The visions always come in my dreams. But they feel real, as real as right now, and ALWAYS in this trailer, not parts and pieces of other scenes like in most dreams. It's like when I go to sleep; I enter another world where we work together to rid humanity of all the scumbags walkin' around free. We are a powerful team, and vengeance is our game."

"So, wait, don't tell me, now you're seeing into the future somehow? That is some fucked-up shit!"

"My mom said somethin' the other day about dreams, and at the time, I didn't pay much attention 'cause she's always goin' on about somethin', you know. Anyway, she said dreams are the mind's way of workin' shit out when you sleep that it can't crack when you're awake. When bad stuff happens in your dreams, there's a good chance it'll happen in life. The trick is to be ready when it happens. I think she's right. We both had terrible things happen that changed us down to the bone. One thing is sure: no one will ever catch me unaware again like Jeff did. And I'm bettin' no one will take advantage of you again either."

Jesse was quiet now, trying to understand everything that had just happened. Sana couldn't tell if she was freaking out or what until she broke the silence.

"So, how do you see this "team" playing out?"

"It's funny. Until I started cuttin' hair at the church, I thought I was the only person with world-class shitty luck. Everybody else was gettin' along without a care in the world. But I noticed somethin' strange happens when someone sits in the salon chair. It's like some invisible wall comes down, and they feel free to unload their deepest, darkest secrets. I don't have to poke or prod to get them started; I jus' have to listen. It happened with you, and it's happened with others. I could tell you tales about women at that church who've endured as much pain as we did, some even more. They even tell me the names of these evil bastards and where they are now. I've seen several of them workin' very nearby, within sight of the church. These women are still terrified of what they might endure if these fuckers tried to create an opportunity."

"I've never thought about it before, but you're right. There's something about being near someone who supplies comfort in such a close and intimate way that opens mouths. I've always done that, and until I had something terrible happen, it didn't matter. We were just prattling away, passing the time, while they worked on my hair."

"So, here's what I think we could do. I'll ID those assholes in a class by themselves and get as much info as possible on where they work and what they look like. Then, you can sort out how we might lure them into your lair here. You're an pretty gal, and since you've had first-hand dealin's with this kind of dirt-bag, you'll know how to push their buttons. I'm guessin' some of them would even find it kinky to have sex in a butcher shop and never see the danger that awaits right inside."

Jesse looked hard at Sana.

"You are a cool and calculating little thing, aren't you? And all this time, I thought you were some quiet, meek little creature, just trying to stay out of trouble."

"That's the key, Jesse. Keep everybody off guard, and never let them see the real you until it's too late."

She walked around the trailer, looking at everything in a new and clarifying light.

"There is one problem though I haven't entirely figured out. Once we get these bastards cut up and whatnot, what do we do with them? We can't sell them to Walmart or the other grocery stores."

It was Jesse's turn to add some dimension to the plan.

"Oh, I can definitely help with that. In my work, I travel all over this area, hundreds of miles in any direction, and I have discovered all kinds of roadside barbecue joints and chicken shacks serving all kinds of crazy shit. Korean, Vietnamese, Thai, Mongolian—you name it. They cook everything from goats to horses, cats, dogs, rabbits, and even snakes. So, something that might look strange to my guy at Walmart would look perfectly normal to them. Then there's the guys with the chicken and pig farms. They are always looking for supplements for their feed, and these animals will eat anything put in front of them. They don't ask too many questions about what's in it, so if I say it's 100% bone meal, that's what it is. That whole 'ignorance is bliss' thing comes in handy sometimes."

"Well then, let's get started. What do you think?"

"I'm in."

CHAPTER 20

Anne could tell by the tentative way she entered the church that this girl had been through hell recently. She wore oversized dark glasses, hair falling over her face, and shuffled her feet like each step was a study in pain. Then there was the oversized raincoat, which, if it had rained in the last six weeks or so, might have made sense but otherwise only served to conceal as much as possible.

She crossed the dining room to greet her.

"Hello, I'm Anne. Welcome."

The girl was very nervous, unsure about everything or how to respond.

"Hi Anne... I'm Elizabeth. No, just Beth. Nobody calls me Elizabeth anymore. Sorry."

"Okay, Beth. Good to meet you. Let's take care of your coat and get you some food."

Beth grabbed at her coat, cinching the collar tight around her neck.

"No! No, I'd rather keep it on. I get cold a lot, and it keeps me warm."

Anne stepped back calmly and guided her to the buffet.

"Okay, no worries. Follow me, and I'll get you a warm plate of food and something cool to drink. You're in luck; we're having meatloaf today.

A real treat."

Beth cautiously followed her to the buffet, casting glances left and right as she proceeded. She tried to be inconspicuous, but that's impossible in a room where everyone knows how to play the game.

She was starving, having had nothing to eat for the three days since she'd run away from her maniacal husband. It took all her willpower not to cram everything in her mouth right there at the buffet. With her tray now full, she turned and scanned the room for an empty table, or at least one that was not so crowded. Two Black ladies were seated near the back, keeping very much to themselves. That looked like a safe bet.

As Beth approached, Sana and Tara took notice of her and began their appraisal, nodding to each other subtly: *Yep, she's one of us.*

"Hi! I'm Tara, and this is my daughter, Sana. Please sit with us. Let us know if we can get anythin' for you."

"Thank you. I'm starving, so if you don't mind, I'd like to eat in peace."

"Sure, sure. We understand completely."

Food had never tasted as good to Beth as it did right then. The last three days of hiding out and running had exhausted her mentally and physically, and when she let her guard fall in this place, she felt safe; she almost wanted to cry. Her plan to leave had been a long time coming, but the catalyst to push her over the top was sudden and unexpected.

She was alone in their apartment. Her husband was out on another late night of drinking and card playing. He had locked her in, as always, when he left, saying, "Can't be too careful around here, you know."

Hours later, she heard him coming up the stairs, pissing and moaning about losing again, only this time, he seemed to have reached an even more pathetic state of loss. And from what she could hear, he wasn't alone. Terrified now, all she could do was wait.

Fumbling with his key to get it into the lock, she finally heard it go "click." Then, Bobby fell into the apartment, pushing the door open. Nate, the stranger with him, laughed, doubled over, thinking this was the funniest site ever and grabbed and set him upright again.

"Dere, she is! I to'd you she weren't much to look at, but she's a good fuck," Bobby mumbled.

Nate lets go of Bobby, and he slowly melted down on the floor again and passed out. Stepping over him, he grabbed Beth by the throat and roughly pulled her to him.

"Ain't you a pretty little thing? Your shit-bag hubby there owes me a whole lotta money, and he offered you up as payment. I don't usually barter, especially on a piece of tail, but I'm feelin' generous tonight."

Then, throwing her down on the sofa, he slapped her hard across the face several times. Grabbing her hair roughly with one hand while he undid his trousers with the other, he proceeded to skull-fuck her as Bobby watched from the floor. After a minute, he knocked her almost unconscious and proceeded to rape her. Time seemed to stand still. She felt as if she had left her body and was seeing the scene from a corner of the ceiling. She saw Nate humping her like a madman, and now Bobby was stirring back to life, but instead of helping free her from this lunatic, he just slumped back into the chair and watched. The fucker even seemed to have an evil smile on his face. When Nate had finally had enough, he did the sweetest thing he could and knocked her out cold. He turned towards Bobby as he pulled his pants back on.

"Well, Bobby, I guess we'll call your debt settled for now. But don't go thinkin' she's gonna to be your bankroll again. And apparently, you've never had a good fuck."

Before he left, he gave him a quick smack upside the head.

"Night loser."

"Can we get you anythin' else? You seem like you haven't eaten in a while," Sana asked when Beth finished her plate.

"No. Thank you. I'm good."

She stood quickly and looked around the room, almost as if she expected trouble to come rushing towards her, and not knowing what else to do, she backed away from the table, turned, and ran back out the door.

Looks like Jesse and I have found our first target.

Tara said, "That child has been through hell. No, I take that back; she's still in hell. She ain't made it through yet."

Anne saw all this play out from her station behind the buffet. It caused her great pain to see these women come in like they did, damaged emotionally and physically, wave after wave, with no seeming change in the tide. If anything, the numbers appeared to be only increasing. And not just the numbers but the trauma levels they brought with them. Some women looked like they had been through an all-out war and barely escaped the battle alive. Every passing day was a test of her faith, a test she felt needed to be reexamined. The path she had been following all these years wasn't up to the task anymore, and she felt in her spirit that something had to change.

CHAPTER 21

Beth finally stopped moving just around the corner from the church, realizing she couldn't keep running like she had for the last three days. She had to trust someone, and if you couldn't trust a church, then who?

Maybe not the best thought, considering some of the stuff she saw on the news about priests diddling little boys, but such is the mind of a battered soul. It wants to believe, even when it shouldn't. Wasn't that how she'd ended up with Bobby? Her friends had warned her, "That boy is no good. You can do better than him. You deserve better than him. Wake up!" She wanted to believe he could change, that all she had to do was love him, and he would become the man she wanted him to be. Instead, he had changed her. His abuse and isolation had destroyed her self-confidence and sense of well-being, replacing it with fear and self-loathing.

She slid down the church wall into a ball, wrapping her arms around her body, and quietly started to cry.

She was startled back to reality when Sana and Tara walked up and spoke to her.

Tara asked, "Beth, sweetie, you okay? What am I asking? Course you ain't okay. Why else would you be here? How can we help?"

"I'm just so tired of it all. I think you know how it is—even better than me." Then, laughing through tears, said, "I'm a hot mess, for sure."

The girls reached down and pulled her up.

"Come with us. We got a little beauty salon right around the corner. You can stay there until you figure out what you want to do next. Okay?" Tara asked.

Sana added, "You could use a bit of babyin'. You'd be amazed how good a shampoo and haircut can make you feel. Come on."

"That sounds great. Thank you," Beth said.

They guided her down the street into the salon.

She sat quietly in the chair while the ladies continued their activities, turning on lights, opening the blinds, starting music, and lining up their scissors and combs.

"Let me hang up your coat, and get you shampooed," Tara said.

Beth hesitated momentarily, then shook her coat off, wincing in pain as she did. When Tara took her coat, she saw severe bruising on Beth's arms and torso; those were just the parts she could see outside her t-shirt. Beth dropped her head and started crying again.

Tara walked over and hugged her gently.

"Child, sweet child, you're gonna to be okay. We got you—no need to shed them tears here. We'll make it all better. You'll see."

Sana walked over and took Beth by the hand.

"Girl, we've been where you've been, so we know exactly what's goin' through your mind—no need to feel shame or any of that other bullshit."

Beth hugged her hard, burying her head against her shoulders, feeling she had been seen and heard for the first time in a long while.

"Thank you both so much. Thank you."

And so, once in the chair, Beth's confessions began to flow.

The baby was active during much of the chatter with Beth, something

Sana was not surprised by. What did surprise her was how the baby seemed to be actively listening in as Beth emptied her bucket of woe, an expression Sana had stolen from Jesse. The baby became especially active and excited when the tale got dark or gruesome.

The worrisome thing for Sana was the object of the baby's excitement. Was it enthusiastic about what the evil man had done, cheering him on in a darkly peculiar way, or was it deeply sympathetic to Beth's case, wanting to exact proportional revenge? She would find no correct answer today, just a keen observation for future context.

Sana held up a mirror for Beth to see her new look.

Again, she broke down and cried, but these tears seemed to come from a happier place.

"It looks great! Really great. I've never known what to do with my hair, and you've sorted out all my cowlicks and whatnot on the first attempt. Thank you!"

Sana brushed the hair clippings away and removed the apron she had draped around Beth. She jumped out of the chair and hugged Sana again.

"You both have been so kind and understanding. I don't know what else to say but 'Thank you.'"

Tara hugged her.

"Beth, when we first met Mrs. Anne over at the church, she told us somethin' that stuck with me. She said, 'I'm investin' in you so you can do the same for someone else soon.' Beth, child, you the recipient of her investment in us. Now, you got to do the same. I can't tell you when or how, but that's how this deal works."

Tara didn't realize that Beth had already done just that, in the form of all the information she and Jesse needed on her dirt-bag of a husband, Bobby. His time on God's green earth was not long. The baby kicked excitedly in apparent agreement.

LOW
AND
SLOW

CHAPTER 22

It'd been a few weeks since his hose-bag of a wife had left him, and Bobby had an itch that needed scratching. So, he popped on a clean pair of Dickies, ran a blob of wax through his hair, checked the mirror twice, and was out the door, his destination for the evening—Bouncin' Betty's.

Even if he couldn't get next to a woman, which would be his first order of business, he could at least cast a lustful glance their way. Tuck a few Washington's in their garters, give them a knowing wink and a nod, and who knows, they might be just lonely and hungry enough to look his way. *A man can hope, can't he?*

Jesse sat calmly at her usual table at Betty's. It was "usual" because she had sat in the same spot all the previous times she'd been to the bar scouting for Bobby.

Having no allegiance to either side of the sexual divide, she viewed the scene through a lens of opportunity; all was fair in love and war to her. This widening of the playing field occurred shortly after she left her deadbeat husband. During that particularly dark period, a kind stranger of similar circumstance offered her every tenderness, and she discovered that she liked it. To her, sex was sex, and it didn't matter one bit about orientation other than the obvious who was making the advances.

What passed for regulars in the bar was a menagerie of harmless characters who flirted with the servers and watched the spectacle from afar. Why waste their hard-earned dollars when someone else's investment made them the same return? It's just good economic sense.

So, when she saw Bobby come strolling into the bar, weaving his way to an empty seat right below the pole at the end of the runway, like a sidewinder in the desert, she knew something special would happen.

The working girls used their telepathic language, and in a nanosecond or less, they signaled that trouble was in their very near future, like an unheard SOS. In this case, SOS meant "Same Old Shit."

Bobby ordered a pitcher of the cheapest beer on tap, and the program started. His first couple of engagements consisted of waving a bill in the air, like a rescue flag, to attract the prey his way. Then, once the target had moved in closer, he slowly pulled the dancer's garter out to nudge a nasty single underneath with a couple of his nicotine-stained fingers. Ending with the obligatory "wink and nod," the message was transmitted. Sadly for him, nothing was received by the intended recipient.

Jesse found this activity humorous and decided to move in for a closer look. She settled in at a high-top table across the runway from Bobby and made her move.

Inviting one of the dancers her way by waving a crisp Lincoln in the air, Bobby couldn't help but notice the exchange.

Both women eyed each other with romantic intent, eyes ablaze and mouths open just so. He was sure he would hear gentle moaning if he could get closer. After the exchange, each settled back into position to await the next phase of the unspoken transaction.

Bobby took a deep gulp of liquid courage and, giving himself a quick stink check under his pits, slid his chair back and walked over to Jesse's table.

She watched in rapt attention, cataloging his every move as he wound through the bar. She could almost see the thought bubble above his head: *You mustn't appear too eager, or you'll spook the prey. You must approach like a panther or some other big jungle cat.*

Deliberately looking away as he approached, Jesse eagerly awaited his opening salvo.

"Well, hey, little lady. I haven't seen you 'round here before. I'm Bobby. Can I buy you a drink? What'll you have?"

"Hey, Bobby. I'm Jesse. I think I'm good for now on the drink, but thanks for asking. I haven't seen you here before either, so maybe we've just missed each other like two ships passing at night."

She winked at that, and Bobby took it as a definite "Let's party!" sign.

"I'm new in town, and this is the first place I've checked out. What else is there to do for a gal who likes to get a little wild?"

Looking around for inspiration, Bobby liked the sound of that.

"You know, there's a place on the edge of town with pool tables and a great jukebox—Billy Joe's Bar and Sir-Loon—I think you'll like it. Why don't we relocate there and see what we can shake loose?"

Jesse looked him straight in the eyes, maintaining contact as she rocked back on the stool and drained her beer in one long gulp.

"Ah! Well, let's go then. I'll follow you. You can't miss my rig. It's the big MOBILE BUTCHERY trailer behind the F-250."

Bobby didn't know how to react to that information, so he stammered as best he could.

"Well, I can't wait to hear more about that. Follow me."

Jesse followed him out into the parking lot and waited to see him pull around to the street. Once on the road, she called Sana and told her to meet at Billie Joe's and look for her trailer in the back. About 15 minutes later, they arrived at the destination.

"Billy Joe's Bar and Sir-Loon" was painted above the door in a ragged paintbrush font. Nice. She couldn't wait to see the lowlifes in here. She pulled around behind the building near what she hoped was the rear exit and parked her rig.

Bobby was nervously waiting for her at the entrance.

She could hear "Free Bird" blaring out of the jukebox. Inside the bar, every square inch of every surface held clues to the previous customer's existence. Signed dollar bills, women's panties, men's briefs, mug shots, newspaper clippings, concert tickets, faded wedding garters—you name it, it was all there. Jesse slowly spun around and took in the scene as Bobby looked on, hoping for a clue.

"Wow, this place is a trip down memory lane. Or maybe it's more like the "Freeway of Love," as she winked at Bobby.

"Come on, I got us a table lined up over here. Let me get you a beer. I'll be right back, so don't you go anywhere."

"I'll be right here, sugar."

Bobby was feeling mighty sure of himself now. Shit, he hadn't lost a step during his time with Beth. If anything, he'd learned a few tricks, and now this little filly was about to see what he could really do. *Just play it cool, and you got this.*

While Bobby was away getting beers, Jesse quickly scanned the bar, looking for the exit door out the back. Bingo! Right at the end of the hall, where the bathrooms were.

Just as Bobby returned to their table, catching his eye, she popped a little white pill on her tongue and asked Bobby if he'd like one.

"Well, why not? I'd hate to see you havin' all the fun without me."

And so she swallowed her minty fresh Tic-Tac while Bobby swallowed his roofie, each washing it down with a long, cold swig of beer. Let the good times roll.

About 15 minutes later, Bobby was well on his way to Neverland. He was stumbling around, and Jesse had to catch him several times, so he didn't fall onto the table next to them.

"Whoa, Bobby, I think you need some fresh air. Let's take this party outside and get you livened back up. Come on."

"Hell yeah! Woohee!"

Jesse sat him down on the trailer's bumper and waited for the last vestige of consciousness to depart. Her wait wasn't long, and when she was sure he was out, she pushed him aside and opened the rear gate. Sana popped out and helped her drag him inside.

"So, this is Bobby? Don't look like much, but we never know, do we?"

"Yep, this is him. He might not look like much, but compared to Beth, he's a giant. Help me get his feet hooked up to this winch."

She zip-tied his feet and hands together and suspended him upside-down in the trailer. Sana saw a drain in the floor just under the hook overhead, and suddenly she knew what it was for.

Bobby was out like a light, even though he was now hanging upside down, feet tied above, and hands tied below.

Then, Jess took a long knife from the wall and cut away all his clothes in one fluid motion. It was a thing of beauty. The only thing left between Bobby and the good Lord were his heavy work boots.

Working quickly now, Jesse slid two shower curtain walls down both sides of the trailer. They created a stall where the only thing visible was Bobby and the floor.

"Okay, he's going to be coming around soon, and when he does, I want his head to explode. Strip down and wait back here with me."

Sana said, "What! I ain't gonna do that. No way."

Jesse turned and looked at her, smiling the most evil smile Sana had ever seen.

"Trust me, Sana. He won't get within a yard of you. He couldn't break free if he tried. Those steel cables and hooks can support an entire cow, so this little fuck is nothing to worry about. And when I'm good and ready, we'll pop him with this, and it's *Adios, muchacho.*"

Jesse held up an overly large strap-on dildo with two small leather holsters on each side, holding her favorite fillet knives. She'd modified the dildo to hide a Captive-bolt (C-bolt for short) stun gun inside.

"It operates on compressed air, like a nail gun, and when I press this button, a four-inch-long bolt will shoot right through old Bobby's brain. He won't feel a thing, now or ever again."

"Damn girl, that's some cold shit right there. But I still don't see what that has to do with me strippin' down."

"If I know this sick fuck like I think I do, he'll get a boner when he sees us making out with each other, even though his ass is hanging upside down in this trailer. He won't be able to help himself. Then, we'll pop him, stiff cock and all."

Sana's baby was kicking like never before during this crazy exchange with Jesse, and she felt she might go into labor, even though that was still a couple of months away.

"So, we gonna make out while this twisted fuck watches hangin' upside down? You crazy, you know."

Then, like clockwork, Bobby started to stir.

Jesse switched on some bump-and-grind music, and they started making out in the dim light at the back of the trailer as Bobby looked on.

Sana's body was a spectacle. The skin on her belly was stretched beyond what he thought possible. Her nipples were dark and as big as silver-dollar pancakes.

Jesse's body was a study of classic beauty. She had well-toned muscles, perky tits, and a perfectly manicured bush. The strap-on dildo/holster combo was something out of the ordinary.

"Hey, what are ya'll doing way over there without me? Get me down from here."

Jesse looked lustfully at him and then slid her hands between Sana's legs, catching her off guard with her gentle touch.

"Aww, you're over there and can't seem to get down. Here, let me see what I can do about that."

Bobby smiled wildly again as she knee-crawled towards him on the floor, ending up with her red-lipped mouth cock-high in response to his growing concern.

Jesse turned and looked at Sana.

"See, I told you he'd rise to the occasion."

Then she reached back, grabbed the C-bolt gun/dildo, and ran it up and down his temple, stroking his face with it.

"Oh yeah, you like this big, hard cock on your skin. I'll bet you'd like to play with something else hard, wouldn't you? Oh, baby. Or maybe you'd rather see me shove this in her mouth, so you can watch like you did when your friend raped your wife."

It took a few seconds for this last bit of information to cut through the fog that was Bobby's brain, but when it hit home, he suddenly got very nervous. Stupidly so.

"What are you talkin' about? What are you bringin' that cow into the party for? She's jus' a whiny bitch. Come on now, get me down from here, and let's have some fun. I ain't never put salt and pepper on my tube steak at the same time before."

Jesse kneeled close enough to press the C-bolt against his head and said as suggestively as possible, "Oh, Bobby! You really know how to push a girl's buttons. Here, let me return the favor."

Then, she pushed the trigger, and he was dead with little more than the sound of a nail gun going off—THWACK. His body didn't twitch a muscle. She was always amazed at the efficiency of this invention.

"Is that it? Is he gone?" Sana asked.

After a few seconds, Bobby's once stiff cock dropped like a parking garage gate.

Jesse stood up and turned to Sana again, looking like her usual self.

"Yep, Bobby is no more, but he is about to be reincarnated. He just won't be coming back as another human being. Let's get started."

The next several hours were a blur.

Jesse quickly dressed, hopped out of the trailer, and drove to a nearby ranch, with Sana following close behind. She knew the ranch owner well and knew he would be out of town taking in a Houston Astros game. He loved baseball and even built a private airstrip so he could fly away anytime he wanted. It must be nice.

On safe ground, they started on the task at hand. Jesse slit Bobby's throat and bled him. They sawed, trimmed, and ground his body into various meat products. Like Sana's dream, she instinctively knew what to do whenever Jesse directed her. Her muscle memory was working perfectly, even though this was the first time actual muscles, other than her brain, had come into play.

Jesse already had a buyer in mind for Bobby, and she was excited to see how this new offering would go over. He was Korean and ran a roadside barbecue stand out in the middle of nowhere. It was one of those off-the-grid places everyone knows about, and without fail, upon their first visit, they asked, "Why in the hell are you out here in the middle of nowhere?" To this day, no one has ever received an answer.

His specialty was galbi, which was typically made with beef short ribs. But since his secret recipe had so many flavors, using marinades, spices, and aging, it's hard to tell it was ever beef. All your mouth knows is that it tastes fantastic. So, swap out beef for Bobby, and no one's wiser. If he asked about the ribs, like what kind of animal is this, she'd say, "Oh, it's a new hybrid, a cross between a goat and a cow." Or hell, she could even say it was a unicorn, and he'd never question it. "The meat is really lean, and the flavor is very delicate. They don't yield a lot of meat, but what they do is very tasty."

The sun was coming up when they popped the back of the trailer open. It felt good to breathe fresh air again and know their work on Beth's account was successful. Her hateful husband would never harm anyone else. Sana was exhausted, but Jesse seemed to be still buzzing.

"Jesse, aren't you wiped after all that? How can you be so wide-eyed and bushy-tailed?"

"Working in my trailer on an animal always gets me stoked, and this particular animal really did the trick. I imagine it's like you when you're cutting hair. Your brain enjoys the routine, and your hands embrace the brief workout, leaving you with a sense of well-being when you finish with the customer."

Sana smiled at that.

"I guess you're right. I'll tell you one thing: this baby was havin' the time of its soon-to-be life while we worked. A couple of times, I felt like I might go into labor right there. That would have been somethin'. At least it's settled back down now."

"Okay, let's hit the road. You gotta get back, and I have to go see a man about some meat."

CHAPTER 23

Anne couldn't help but notice the profound change in Beth. She'd become friends with Sana and Tara and even let them spruce her up a bit. She was working hard in the kitchen, and time seemed to be healing her mental and physical wounds. Anne walked over to where she was setting up drinks for the lunch crowd.

"Hi, Beth. How are you doing? You are looking really well."

"Hey, Anne. I am good, really good. So much better than when you first saw me. 'A hot mess' doesn't quite do it justice. But thanks to your kindness and others here, I'm in a much better place now."

"Well, you've certainly pulled yourself together. Thank you for your hard work here at the church. Your investment in others will pay huge dividends in the future. Ultimately, we control how we spend our time, and I feel helping others is the best way to invest."

"Sana and Tara told me about your 'investments' in people. I didn't understand at first what they were talking about when they said you invested in them. But now I see what they meant. The girls are so easy to talk to and, sadly, have walked in my shoes, so when they tell me things will turn out okay, I can't help but believe it. They are living proof."

"Sana and Tara are two extraordinary ladies indeed. They were very different people than the two you see working in the salon today. They were very wary of me and others when they first arrived. But we all need help along the way to succeed. I don't know how exactly, but your connection will help them move on from their past, just like they've helped you."

"I think you're right about that."

Walking around the dining hall, she felt that everything was under control. She could loosen up, follow her advice, and see the girls about some pampering. It would do her some good to get away, even if only for an hour or so.

Tara saw Anne walk by the storefront just before she opened the door, so she greeted her with a hug when she stepped inside.

"Well, hello, stranger. What brings you by today?"

Anne smiled as she released her.

"I thought I would follow my own advice for a change and let you girls pamper me a bit. It's been a long time since I've had a new 'do,' so let's see what kind of magic you can work."

"Alrighty then, let's get you shampooed, and I'll see what we can make happen," Sana said.

And just like that, as Tara gently shampooed Anne's head, massaging the lather into her hair, and Sana listened in, the walls came down.

First, Anne talked about working at the church. How long she'd been there, the challenges along the way, the difficult parishioners who "talk the talk but don't walk the walk."

Then, as Sana dried her hair with a towel and combed out the tangles, the conversation shifted, and Anne's distant past debuted, and the trauma she endured all those years ago returned as fresh as if it had just happened.

"Congratulations! You're pregnant," the nurse said.

"No, I can't be. No, no, I just can't be," Anne said nervously.

"Oh, I take it this wasn't a planned pregnancy then?"

"Absolutely not! It was a stupid one-night fling. I barely know the guy."

"Well, you caught it early enough that you have options. You could get an abortion, or you could carry it to term and put it up for adoption."

"Oh God, why did this happen? Why?!"

Then, the conversations between her parents and the boy's parents tested her faith in ways she could never imagine.

Her father said, "Anne, you know I'm not a believer in abortion, but you can't possibly think of keeping the baby."

"Of course not," Anne said.

Her mom was silently distraught.

But the boy's parents were insistent.

"Absolutely not! How can you even consider having an abortion? God will punish you forever if you do such a thing," his father said.

"Anne, we could help care for you and the baby and adopt it through the church when it arrives," his mother said.

The boy stared into space, seeing his once-promising future fade like a heavy fog burning off.

Ultimately, all these good intentions and well-laid plans were little more than high-quality paving material for the highway to hell.

So here she was, young, unmarried, and pregnant. Definitely not the best scenario for a long and happy life. The baby came early, catching everyone by surprise. He was little, but other than that, he seemed healthy. The boy and his parents decided to adopt the child and raise him. When the time came, they would tell him he was one of those "postscript babies" that sometimes catch older couples by surprise. She and the baby's father had no relationship besides what the child needed, so she cut the cord, literally and figuratively, after the adoption.

She moved on as best she could, but in a small town, everyone knows your past and won't let you forget it—the knowing glances, the pitying looks, the whispered innuendo that didn't loosely resemble the truth.

Then, as if fate were playing some twisted form of Russian Roulette with her life, she learned that a drunk driver killed her adopted son and his entire family in a car wreck outside of town, within eyesight of the bar the driver had left just seconds before.

Shocked by this horrible revelation, Sana stopped what she was doing and slowly spun Anne around in the chair so she could see her straight on.

"Oh my god, Anne, I'm so sorry to hear all that. I can only imagine how bad that must have been. No, I take it back; I can't imagine it. It's just too much."

Anne was crying openly, letting the years of pent-up rage, anger, and frustration out. Tara and Sana wrapped their arms around her and joined in, tears falling on Anne's shoulders like a gentle rain. After a few minutes, they collectively caught their breath and started talking again.

Anne settled down.

"Oh god, it felt so good to get that off my chest! I've never told anyone that story before. When I moved away shortly after, I swore I would put all that business in the rear-view mirror. But that's a lie we tell ourselves to get through the immediate break. Tragedy never lets you rest or forget. It's always there, lurking just below the surface, and all it takes is to close your eyes for one second and make the mistake of trying to remember, and your mind will accommodate. It never forgets. Never."

Sana gathered herself.

"You know, you're right. We can't forget the bad shit that happens to us. And bad shit takes on many forms. For you, it was a choice you didn't want, put on you by people who thought they knew better. But even if you had done what your parents wanted, *that memory* would be the shit that haunts you. Different people would be affected, like your friends and family, but you, YOU, would still be fucked up!"

Tara gave Sana a stern look, followed by a subtle nod.

Tara said, "Anne, thank you for sharin' your story with us. That kind of shit will eat you up from the inside if it don't eventually get out. I know you're wonderin' about our situation; what exactly are we doin' here? You'd be somethin' other than human if you wasn't curious. So, since we have entered a kind of sacred sisterhood, I'm gonna share some of our past lives with you. I expect some of it will only confirm what you already thinking, but I'd bet some will scare you to death. You ready?"

Anne took a deep breath.

"I'm as ready as I'll ever be."

As Tara unfurled their past, sparing no details, Sana finished cutting and styling Anne's hair. Then she moved on to her fingernails, and by the time Tara finished speaking, she'd even done a pedicure.

Sana spun Anne around in the chair so they could see her fully. She was transformed. Her hair and very being seemed lighter and brighter; the great weight she had shed in the chair was gone, and Anne was resurrected. She stood up, grabbed them both, and pulled them close.

"Thank you both for saving me today. When I walked in, this was the last thing I expected to receive, but it was precisely what I needed. I didn't realize until I unburdened myself how heavy the past weighed on my soul. And for what? So, thank you for the tears and the ears."

After Anne left, Sana turned to Tara and said, "I'm glad you told her about our past. It feels good to spread that load around a bit. You okay?"

Tara frowned and said, "Yeah, I'm okay, but I get the feelin' there's somethin' you ain't sharin' with me, like where you was last night."

Sana dropped her chin and smiled up at her.

"Nothin' gets past you, ever. One day, I'll share last night with you, but that day isn't today. I'm dog-tired between last night and this morning's drama and need a long nap."

"Okay, baby. I'll put up the 'Closed' sign so you can rest. I got you."

Sana's head barely hit the pillow before she was asleep. And then the dreams came, and the baby danced.

CHAPTER 24

The alarm went off at 5:30 a.m. The murder of crows in the nearby trees started with their morning racket. The sky was a dull gray; rain was a definite possibility, maybe even a thunderstorm. Anne had a bad feeling; it wasn't just the weather forecast. All morning, she'd had a sense of dread. Of course, this was nothing new. She had this feeling often; it's just that things for her and the church family had been going somewhat drama-free as of late, and she hated to think that might come to an end.

Anne saw him first from her position at the end of the serving line. She could tell right away this guy would be trouble; the only question was, what kind?

She approached him and said, "Can I help you?"

Nate turned, looked at her, and did a quick appraisal.

"I'm not sure. I'm looking for a friend of mine's wife."

Then, as only lousy luck would have it, Beth walked out of the kitchen right then, and Nate spotted her.

"Oh, there she is. Excuse me."

Anne watched as he made a beeline to Beth. She could tell by Beth's reaction that this was someone she did not want to see. Ever.

"What are you doin' here? You shouldn't be here," Beth said.

"That's no way to treat an old acquaintance, especially after our last good time," Nate said menacingly.

Beth was visibly shaking now.

"You need to leave here. Now!"

"Oh, I intend to do just that, but I need a little information from you before I split. Your shit-bag husband has run up another debt, and now it seems he's skipped town. You wouldn't happen to know where I might find him? I'd hate to have to count on you to settle his affairs again."

Beth looked at him in total fear and then said as calmly as she could, "I haven't seen Bobby in weeks. I left him the day after your last visit. For all I know, he's dead, left town, or you killed him. The truth is, I don't know and don't care. He's dead to me, no matter what. Now, again, please get out of here and kindly leave me alone."

Anne appeared.

"Beth, is everything okay over here?"

Nate slowly turned and gave her a menacing look. "Yeah, everything is just hunky dory. I'll be seein' you ladies. You take care now."

As he slowly walked away, Beth all but collapsed on the floor. Anne grabbed her up and steered her back into the kitchen.

"Beth, who was that man? Is he your husband?"

Beth looked at her, trying to understand what Anne had just asked.

"No, no! He's definitely not my husband! But he knows my husband, and not in a good way. His name is Nate, and he's a bad, bad man. I'm not safe here now. He's lookin' for my husband, who owes him money again. The last time Nate came lookin' for money, he raped me. In my own home. WHILE MY SHIT-BAG HUSBAND WATCHED!"

By now, Beth had lost control and was yelling and swinging her fists in the air.

Anne had seen these mental breaks before, so she grabbed Beth and held her as tightly as possible, trying to keep her from self-harm. Her anger was so great and all-consuming that it was all Anne could do to keep a grip on her. After a few minutes, Beth started crying deeply, gasping tears, and sank into a puddle on the floor. Anne sat on the floor with her, cradled her, and rocked her like a baby. After a few minutes, she calmed down enough to speak again.

"I'm sorry, Anne. That man is the devil himself. I thought I was safe here, but that's no longer true. I've got to get away from here. Now!" Then, she started crying again, "Oh god, what am I gonna to do?"

Anne pulled her up.

"Well, let's start by getting some fresh air," she said, putting her arm around Beth and steering her outside. "Let's visit Sana and Tara and see what they think. It'll do you good to talk with them."

Sana and Tara were returning from an errand when they saw Anne and Beth approaching. They could immediately tell all was not well.

"Hey, Anne, Beth. You okay? What's wrong?" Tara asked.

"Can we talk in your shop for a bit? Beth had a visitor today, and it's got her concerned for her safety," Anne said.

"Sure, come in, come in," Sana said, quickly shuffling them inside.

As they entered, Sana and Tara locked glances that said: *NOT GOOD.*

They sat Beth in the salon chair and got her something to drink.

Then she replayed the scene in the dining hall. Much of the tale was a retelling for Sana and Tara of what Beth had shared before, but it was new information for Anne. The new debt Bobby had run up with Nate was different, but not surprisingly.

Anne asked, "What do you know about this guy? If I knew who he was, I could talk with the police about a restraining order of some sort."

Beth freaked at this suggestion.

"No, no! I don't want to do anything to give him a reason to see me again. Please! Just help me find somewhere else to go. He's an evil man, and the police won't be able to watch him or his people all the time."

Sana tried to calm her down.

"Okay, okay. We'll have to set up our own watch here until we figure out somethin' else. Let's back up a sec. You know his name is Nate, and your husband owes him money. From gamblin', drugs, or what exactly?"

Beth hung her head, exasperated.

"If I had to guess, I'd say all the above, but I really don't know. Bobby started runnin' with Nate a while back, and suddenly he had money to gamble with, and that's when the trouble started. Like the old song, 'If it wasn't for bad luck, the fucker would have no luck at all.' I don't know if Bobby was helpin' sell drugs or what, but somehow, he managed to get into serious debt to Nate, and that's where I entered the picture. Bobby used me to settle his debt. God, I hate that asshole."

Tara looked at Sana to see how she reacted to this exchange. She could tell by Sana's calm demeanor that she knew much more about Bobby than she was letting on. And she would find out exactly what as soon as Beth and Anne left.

Anne said, "Okay, let me do some digging with my network and see what we can find out. In the meantime, Beth, you stay out of sight at the church. There is no need to make his accessing you easier by having you work in the dining room, so keep your head down and your eyes open. And let us know ASAP if you think of anything else to help us find this guy. Okay?"

"I'm sorry, guys. Honestly, I am. I never had any idea that guy would find me here."

"That's okay, baby. Now that we know he's up to no good, we know better what kind of trouble we dealin' with, even if we don't know exactly who he is," Tara said.

Anne pulled Beth out of the chair and left, heading back towards the church.

They had no sooner cleared the storefront window when Tara turned to Sana.

"So, tell me how you know this Bobby so well. I could tell by that look on your face when Beth was talkin' about where he might be and what he might be doin' that you knew exactly where he was and what he was doin'. Don't lie to me, girl; I know you."

Sana calmly stood behind the salon chair.

"Okay, I think it's time I come clean, but it's gonna to take a while. So why don't you put out that 'Closed' sign, and let's go for a ride? That way, no one walks in by surprise."

Tara stood, walked to the door, and flipped the sign.

"You want me to drive or ride shotgun?" Tara asked.

"Shotgun, of course."

A loud thunderclap popped as soon as they stepped outside.

CHAPTER 25

When Anne pulled into the driveway, David was busy working under a big Mack truck rig. He looked up and thought: *Now what?*

She momentarily gathered herself in the car, trying to figure out how best to approach David with this latest ask. Instinctively, she felt he might bristle at what she was about to request. She took a deep breath, lowered her head, and entered the shop.

"Hey, David. I hate to show up like a bad penny, but I really need to talk to you about something. And no, it doesn't involve swapping a car or anything like that. I need some 'ear to the ground' kind of dirt."

David smiled uneasily and wiped his hands on a shop rag.

"Okay. I wasn't makin' much headway on this old, worn-out bulldog anyway. Come on."

They walked to his office in the back of the shop. Just getting to it was like walking through a hoarder's paradise. Junk of every description was stacked ceiling high, and the path was little more than shoulder wide. Anne felt dirty just walking through it all. The office was a little better, and thankfully, it had air conditioning. She noticed a ratty old computer and monitor with several security camera feeds displayed.

"So, what kind of dirt are we talking about?"

"First, thank you in advance for any help you can give me. I know I ask a lot of you. I'm trying to track down an individual. I don't have much info on him besides a first name and a rough idea of what he's involved in."

"Which is?"

"His name is Nate, and we think he's involved with selling drugs or running a gambling operation. One of my gals had a nasty run-in with him before she left her loser of a husband. Now, he's tracked her down, looking for the husband who owes him money and threatening her. I won't go into all the details, but let me say, this guy is terrible."

David rubbed his three-day-old beard and scratched his chin.

"Yeah, he's a piece of shit if there ever was one. I know several local idiots who've joined his 'gang,' if you can call it that. He's involved in selling bootleg fentanyl and other drugs, plus God knows what else. His scam is pretty basic. First, he gets these idiots with an IQ of my boot size to start usin' drugs. Then, once they're higher than a kite, he gets them gamblin', and of course, they always lose. Next thing you know, they're runnin' shit all over the place for him. These guys come to me and ask if I can hop up their rigs or add booby-trap shotguns and other shit like that. You do not want to fuck with these guys; pardon my French."

Anne looked at him with wide eyes.

"Wow! I could tell he was terrible, but my radar must be rusty, as I had no idea he was that evil. So, is he a local? I've never seen him before, but I'm not running around looking for drugs or anything like that."

"I don't know exactly where he lives, but one of the knuckleheads let it slip one day that his warehouse is the next county over. It used to be a Dollar General store. There was a mysterious fire one night, and curiously, rather than repair it, the corporate geniuses at DG decided to build a new store just around the corner, within eyesight of the first one. It makes no sense to me, but hey, I'm just a grease monkey turnin' wrenches."

"Okay, that gives us something to work on. Thank you so much for your time and the information. I appreciate you more than you know."

"You're welcome, but please, Anne, do not go messin' with this guy. You have enough dark shit at the church without stirrin' up this asshole."

They both stood to go, and Anne hugged David.

"Thanks again. I'll be careful, don't you worry."

As she pulled away from the shop, it suddenly became clear what all the controversy had been about last year concerning the Dollar General stores.

Folks in the next county were all up in arms because they were building so many dollar stores, some of them literally within eyesight of another one. Property values were falling, and these stores attracted folks that didn't fit their description of 'desirable.' The mayor had hired a PR firm from outside to make the whole mess quietly disappear, and they earned their money because they quashed the story in a matter of days. Then, there was a mysterious fire at one of the older stores. It didn't cause that much damage, so people were more than surprised when they built a brand-new store just down the street. And guess who owned the new property? None other than Mr. Mayor.

She headed to the local paper to see if the reporter who had covered the ruckus could shed some light on the matter. With any luck, there would be some interesting background that didn't make it into the story. At a minimum, she could put a period at the end of this path if it leads nowhere.

CHAPTER 26

Just after midnight, the U-Haul cargo van pulled into the loading area behind the burnt-out Dollar General. Nate hit the button that rolled up the large garage door. As it squeaked and moaned, he motioned the driver inside and put the door down again once the truck cleared the threshold. Then, like fire ants coming out of a kicked-over hill, his band of misfits started unloading the truck.

"Any trouble makin' the drop?" Nate asked the new guy.

"Nope, everything was just like you said. Easy in, easy out."

He handed a small duffel bag to Nate, who opened it and did a quick tally of the contents.

"Perfect. That's what I like to hear. Okay, let's break these boxes down and make up the next batch."

He headed to his makeshift office in the corner of the warehouse and sent a cryptic text message. "New marketing materials arrived. When/where is the next sale?"

The phone on his bedside table lit up and silently buzzed. The mayor rolled over, read the note, and typed back a "handshake" emoji.

Nate saw the response and smiled.

"Good old mayor. Always doing the people's work, 24/7."

He had to give him credit; the guy knows how to work a crowd. And when the shit hit the fan about building all the dollar stores, he nipped the story in the bud. A little PR money here, a little payoff there, and the next thing you know, all's quiet on the Western front.

Of course, there were always those self-righteous souls who wouldn't take a payoff, but after a little unfriendly persuasion, even they came around to see the light.

He had lost two guys in the last couple of months. Just disappeared without a trace.

These disappearances were causing him concern. It wasn't that these guys were irreplaceable. Hardly. With things the way they were these days, he could drive around town and, in less than 15 minutes, have a whole new crew hopping out of his truck. The trouble was, these new guys were the same ones he was selling to, so he knew they would be worthless, even if they were in ample supply.

No, the worrying thing about these disappearances was the absolute quiet surrounding them.

Jeff was never the brightest guy but knew how to keep his head down, especially with his old man locked up in the pen.

Bobby was the same, although he did have that nagging wife of his to deal with, so that could be part of it. He had put the fear of God in her, so she shouldn't be a problem anymore.

That nosy wench at the church might become a problem, but nothing he hadn't seen before.

His phone buzzed again.

"Media plan for the new campaign to follow. Stand by."

It was convenient that the mayor was also a pharmacist. That made the whole "illegal drugs" game pretty simple. He'd write up a large order for all his stores and have them shipped to a locale nearby. And having a brother-in-law who owned a bunch of Walgreen's in several states didn't hurt either. They just washed the drugs through these channels and took the clean cash that came out on the other side.

The Dollar General stores offered an endless supply of users who were easily separated from their hard-earned cash.

Nate learned early on that if he kept his end of the bargain up with the mayor, any scams he ran on the side were hunky dory. Gambling was a natural progression for most of these guys. Many of these poor souls considered buying lottery tickets contributing to their "retirement account," so falling prey to a card game just showed "diversity" within their portfolios. Collecting from these characters was not without its downside, but even that had some appeal. Take Bobby's wife, for example. That Bobby thought she could settle his debt and not run off afterward was unbelievable. It makes a man lose faith in humanity. He chuckled at this last bit. *Nate, you're a twisted fuck.*

CHAPTER 27

The long stretch of two-lane blacktop shimmered with heat. Even though it was mid-morning, it had to be 105º in the shade. The cows and sheep jostled for position under anything that provided shade. So far, it seems the cows were winning.

As Jesse rolled to a stop at her destination, she could see Kim Chee, as she nicknamed her soon-to-be client, holed up in his tin-roofed shack. He was aimlessly humming a tune and mopping ribs with a short-handled mop, smoking a hand-rolled cigarette, the contents of which she was pretty sure were not tobacco-related. Sweet-smelling hickory smoke wafted across the exposed beam roof and rolled out the window screens from there.

She walked up and knocked "shave-and-a-haircut" on the screen door. It was very early, so customers hadn't started lining up yet.

"Hello! Is anybody home?"

An old, spalted hound of an indeterminate breed slowly walked out to inspect the visitor. He wore a beat-up old collar with the name "LUCKY" stamped on his tin ID plate. Jesse stooped down to rub the dog's chin and laughed when she saw the nameplate.

"Ha! You are a lucky boy. I bet you get the best scraps ever. We should all be so lucky."

When she stood again, she noticed Kim Chee quietly standing beside the homemade 55-gallon drum smoker, smoking and watching.

"We not open yet. Come back later," Kim said, turning his attention back to the smoker. He pulled a handful of hickory chips from a bucket where they were soaking and threw them into the fire pit.

"Yes, I can see you're not open yet. I'm a butcher. I have some freshly butchered meat and other goodies I'd like to show you."

Kim looked at her, confused.

Jesse pointed at the smoker.

"Meat? Ribs? Uhm, Galbi?"

At this last hint, his face lit up, and he said something so quick and foreign that Jesse didn't understand. She took whatever he spoke as a sign that he was interested.

"Wait here. I'll be right back."

She turned and ran back to her trailer, opened the gate, and pulled out the special pack of ribs she and Sana had prepared. When she turned around, she noticed Kim had followed her and was staring into the back of her trailer.

"You live here, in crazy house?"

Jesse laughed.

"No, no. I'm a mobile butcher," she said, pointing to her cow and pig diagrams showing where to make cuts. "This 'crazy house' is my workshop. I travel to ranches and butcher animals for the owners on their property. Sometimes, they pay me in meat."

She held up some of her knives, the saws, and finally, the package of meat for Kim to inspect.

He took the package, confused about what to do with it. Then Jesse helped him unwrap it, revealing the Bobby short ribs. As he recognized what it was, his face lit up.

"Ah, Galbi! You want me cook?"

"Yes, yes! I was hopin' you could try it and tell me how you liked it. If you like, I have more."

Kim nodded profusely.

"Come back later. Tomorrow morning, we try."

Jesse shook her head in agreement.

"Okay, great! One more thing."

She grabbed a package of her specialty sausage and handed it to him.

"This is remarkable ground meat. It's my special recipe. It would make great burgers. I think you'll like this meat very much. Very lean, tender, and tasty. I'll see you tomorrow, okay?"

Kim Chee shuffled away, waving her goodbye over his shoulder.

After meeting with Kim, Jesse felt rather good about her prospects. She closed the trailer and decided to head back into town. She needed to check in with Sana to make sure she was okay. That night they shared with Bobby was wild, even by Jesse's standards. Meeting Sana taught her that you can never judge people by what you see on the outside. It's what's deep down in the dark that counts.

There is something cathartic about riding long stretches of highway. It gives a girl time to think. No one interrupts your concentration. Lately, she'd been concentrating on what she and Sana were now into.

Sana had opened her eyes to just how big the problem was with domestic violence between partners. The thought that this kind of shit happened all the time filled her with a low-boiling rage. But she had to admit, the high she felt after dispatching old Bobby was pretty fucking incredible. Better than any sex she'd ever had. But then, she thought, like sex, any habit can get your ass in a lot of trouble if you aren't careful.

As she rolled through town, she noticed the "Closed" sign hanging in the window at the salon. She pulled into the church parking lot, parked the rig, and headed into the church. As Jesse approached, she saw Anne was setting up tables.

"Hey, Anne, I'm Jesse, a friend of Sana's. I see the 'Closed' sign on the shop. Do you know where they might be? I need to catch up with her on some stuff."

"I'm sorry, I don't. I saw them earlier today. We had a bit of an incident this morning with one of the other girls, and they helped me sort through some things."

Jesse looked startled, not knowing what exactly had happened but feeling connected to it somehow. Hopefully, Bobby wasn't the source of the trouble.

"I'm sorry to hear that. Is everyone okay now?"

"Yes, yes. Well, as good as can be expected. One of the girls had an unexpected, and very much unwanted, visitor, and it upset her terribly. We're taking precautions to keep her safe."

"That's horrible. Is there anything I can do?"

Anne didn't know Jesse well, at least not well enough to confide too much in her, so she knew this was an empty request, made more for show than anything.

"I appreciate the offer, but we're as good as possible. I'll tell the girls you stopped by when I see them."

Jesse left, ran to her truck, and, once inside, texted Sana, "YO! Where are you? We need to talk." Then, thinking that might freak her out, she texted, "All good here. I hope you are safe."

Sana had to give it to her mom. She was one cool customer.

As Sana spun her tale of dreams and visions and the baby's reactions to events, Tara stared intently at her. And when she got around to the undoing of Bobby—how she and Jesse had lured him into her trailer and then butchered him and packaged him for sale at a Korean BBQ stand—she was even more focused. It freaked Sana out a little.

"I knew somethin' was happ'nin' with you. That baby inside you is the devil, sure as I'm sittin' in this car. He couldn't help but be bad; look where he came from." Then she laughed uncomfortably, "Ha, I'm callin' it a him. Hell, all I know is it could be a bad-ass she-devil. Either way, it's controllin' your mind and body. You see that, right?"

"Of course, I see that. How could I not? But there's more to it than that. Just like you knew Jeff would come to the trailer that night, I can see trouble comin' before it hits the horizon. When I hear the stories the women tell me about these assholes, it's like my brain catalogs their shit and helps me see a way to lure them in. I can't explain it. It's like knowin' how to breathe without ever having learned. It just happens."

"That proves you got the devil in you right there. Say no more! And what did Jesse say when you told her all this shit? She freak?"

"No, well, not exactly. We were talkin' in her trailer, and I told her the same story I just shared with you, and she did freak out a little bit. But then the baby got active, so I put her hands on my belly, and Jesse had an incredible vision. This is the part when *I* almost freaked out. In her vision, she was at our trailer the night we killed Jeff. She was pullin' the trigger on the shotgun, only she wasn't shootin' at Jeff; she was shootin' at her ex-husband. It was crazy."

Tara just shook her head. "Lord, have mercy."

They rode silently for a few minutes but were interrupted by Jesse's text. Sana looked at the phone.

"It's Jesse. She wants to talk. Are you okay with heading back?"

"Child, I'm as alright as I'm ever gonna to be. Let's go."

Sana pulled over and texted her back.

"We're good. Headed back now. Meet at the salon in 15 minutes."

The ride back home seemed surreal to Sana, as she had shared all her secrets with Tara, and everything still seemed okay. Only when the baby started kicking wildly did she begin to think otherwise.

CHAPTER 28

As Anne pulled up in front of the newspaper, it suddenly dawned that she no longer had a fresh contact. The reporter she once knew had moved on to bigger and better things, and she hadn't needed to make a new connection until now.

She checked in at the receptionist's desk.

"Hi, I'm not sure exactly who to ask for. I'm seeking help on a story the paper ran a while back, over a year ago. It was about the Dollar General stores in the next county."

The receptionist clicked her tongue, smiled scornfully, signaling her extreme disinterest, and punched the phone to ring the editor.

"Hey, I've got someone here who wants to follow up on a story about a Dollar General story. Can you help her?" She listened briefly as the editor responded, then said, "Okay, I'll send her back. The editor will meet you in the conference room. Follow me."

As she waited in the conference room, she read all the big stories the paper had chosen to display. Some went as far back as the Vietnam War. The most recent had to do with the January 6 insurrection. What a goat rodeo that was.

The editor knocked on the door and entered.

"Hello, I'm William Morrow, the editor here at the paper."

"Hello, William. I'm Anne Madison. Before we get started, I want to thank you for your time. I appreciate it."

"So, what exactly are you looking for? The receptionist said you were interested in the Dollar General story. That's hardly a big scandal. Or do you know something we don't?"

"Let me tell you why I'm starting there. I run a mission down at the Baptist church, helping mainly battered women, but lately, people who COVID-19 has displaced. Anyway, a terrible person visited one of my women yesterday. This person, along with her deadbeat husband, is the reason she ran away. She doesn't know who he is exactly, and all we've been able to piece together is that he's running an illegal drug trade and a gambling operation. We also got word that his base is the old, burned-out Dollar General store the next county over. I remembered the story in the paper about the fire and another store being built down the street. It was one of those stories that's hotter than a match one minute and the next, poof, it's like it never was. So, I figured I'd start there."

"I remember that story well. It started with the locals getting all up in arms when they built the first store. They said it would reduce their property values and attract the wrong demographic. Then, a mysterious fire caused some damage but was hardly a total wreck. But instead of repairing that store, DG decided to build another one, literally within eyesight of the first one. That's when the shit hit the fan. We started digging into who owned the stores, but they hired a PR firm to bury the story before we could get far. We got the owner's name by using the Freedom of Information Act. The properties belong to the mayor over there. I guess he didn't want this news to affect his re-election campaign."

"I can see why he'd want the story to disappear, but why build another store? That doesn't make sense unless he's using the old store for something not above board. Is the reporter who broke the story still working here?"

"I'm sorry, he's not. He moved on not long after the story blew out."

"Do you have any contact information for him? I want to talk with him and see if he has any notes or recollections that might help. Oh, I almost forgot, the guy's name we're looking for is 'Nate.'"

Anne noticed a subtle but definite reaction from William.

"I'm sorry, Anne. We can't give out that information."

Anne felt something was suddenly off about this conversation, so she decided to cut it off.

"Well, thanks again for your time. I appreciate it."

Back in her car, she tried to piece together what had just transpired. At first, the editor seemed to want to help, but he suddenly clammed up when she mentioned Nate's name. She had a bad feeling about this.

As William watched Anne get into her car and leave, he thought he'd better contact the mayor and tell him he had a potential problem headed his way. These church do-gooders were a persistent lot, even if they were misguided in their way of thinking.

William texted.

"Bible thumper, digging around DG1. Big dog is attracting unwelcome attention. Yank leash."

After a few minutes, his burner phone buzzed in his desk drawer. William picked up and looked at the mayor's message.

"Border Cafe at 5:00."

William punched "End."

"Here we go."

Anne pulled back into the church parking lot just as Sana and Tara exited their car. She hopped out of the car and signaled for them to wait.

"Hey ladies, do you have a few minutes to talk? I just returned from the paper and have more information on our problem."

"Sure. Let's go to the salon," Sana said.

As they rounded the corner, Jesse passed back by on the street. She stopped, rolled down the window, and yelled to Sana.

"Hey, let me park this rig, and I'll be right there."

Sana gave her a "thumbs up."

"She stopped by earlier today looking for you. Is she a friend of yours?"

"Yes, we met a couple of weeks ago and hit it off. Jesse is a good person; sadly, she's one of us."

"Oh, sorry to hear that."

They entered the salon, turned on the lights, and settled around the main salon chair. Jesse arrived, and Sana gave her the nod to leave the "Closed" sign out. Jesse locked the door behind her.

Anne took a few minutes to gather her thoughts.

"Okay, I've been digging on our guy. First, I went to see David, who always has an ear to the ground for news. He doesn't know who Nate is, but he knows he's running his operation out of an old Dollar General store in the next county. There was a big story about these stores a while back. People were up in arms about it, and then, 'poof,' it disappeared. So, I went by the paper to see if there was more to learn. The reporter who broke the story wasn't there, so I spoke with the editor. He told me the mayor over there owns these stores. The editor felt the mayor didn't want the story to hurt his re-election campaign, so he hired a PR firm to squash it. The editor initially seemed inclined to be helpful, but his attitude quickly changed when I mentioned Nate's name."

"Damn Anne, you like a dog with a bone," Tara said. "I'd hate to have you lookin' into my shit."

Sana followed: "You've been busy, no doubt. So, let's look at what we know. You've seen this guy, so you could pick him out of a crowd. We think he's runnin' his operation out of this DG store in the next county. And we know Beth's husband, Bobby, was involved with him somehow."

"Wait, how do we know that?" Anne asked, surprised.

"Beth told us her story about Bobby and Nate, the whole awful thing."

Jesse listened intently, as she knew where this conversation was going.

"And now, because of your diggin', we know the mayor is connected somehow to Nate. From what you said about the editor at the paper, he's also connected to the mayor and maybe Nate," Sana continued.

"Okay, so we have these connections, but what can we do with them?"

"Well, that depends on what you think we should do with them. You feel going to the police isn't a possibility, or you'd have gone there first. So that leaves us to take matters into our own hands. Do we want to keep an eye on him somehow and hope he doesn't return, or do we want to devise another plan to ensure he doesn't return?"

At this, Anne looked very concerned.

"What exactly are you saying? We somehow take this guy out. A guy who's running a drug ring and is into gambling and god knows what else. This guy is bad. I do not see how we do that."

Tara, who was typically quiet until now, stepped into the conversation.

"Well, Anne, I think you jus' told us what you'd like to see, even if you didn't quite put it that way. The guy is bad. We've ALL been victims of bad people like him, some way worse than others, but in the end, they was ALL BAD. But you know what? We still here. So, we shouldn't be talkin' about how bad he is, but what we're gonna do about it. What *we* gonna do about it."

Jesse broke her silence.

"I have an idea, but I have some questions first. When Nate came to see Beth, who did he see? Anne and Beth. Anyone else?"

"That's it. Sana and Tara were out, so it was just us two," Anne said.

"Okay, so that makes you the only one out of this group who can ID him. It also means he could identify you, so you can't snoop around his backyard. But I could. He doesn't know me from Adam. I could pop by there under the guise of trying to do some business and see what I can learn. If I can ID him, we can move on to bigger plans."

By now, Anne felt she was the only one in this group who wasn't entirely in the know.

"Okay, it seems all of you know something I don't. You've got to come clean with me right now. I thought we had a 'Sacred Sisterhood' working."

Sana looked at Tara and Jesse, and they all gave her the nod.

"Okay, Anne, you're right. It's time to come clean, but I need you to sit quietly while I tell this tale. There'll be plenty of time later for questions. Agreed?"

Anne looked around and took a deep breath.

"Agreed."

So, for the next hour, she took Anne down the rabbit hole Sana and Jesse now inhabited. Anne listened intently, raising her eyebrows at specific parts of the story—the only emotion displayed. When Sana finally finished, she asked Anne if she had any questions for her or the group.

Anne stood slowly and walked around the room. She wasn't freaked out and didn't seem afraid. She was sorting through a lot of information.

"First off, thanks for telling me all that. It's quite a lot to take in. It makes me think of that phrase about 'faith,' where you firmly believe in something for which there is no proof. I've been thinking a lot recently about how bad people always manage to skirt away somehow. They do these awful things and are never brought to bear for them. It makes me so angry. And now it seems you have come along at just the right time to strengthen my faith in humanity. I know it's unbelievable to say this, but I'm in. I want us to stop this evil once and for all."

The plan was simple. Jesse would visit Nate at the DG, verify she had her man, and she'd take him out if the opportunity presented itself. If it didn't, she'd report back to the group, and they'd make another plan.

CHAPTER 29

Jesse had come up with what she thought was a deliriously twisted plan to engage with Nate and his gang. She would drive out to meet Kim Chee and see how he liked the new ribs, feeling more than confident he would. Then, after her dealings there were complete, she would take some of these freshly smoked ribs on her trip to scout for Nate and use them to engage with his guys. No man can resist a smoky rack of ribs, especially when a pretty girl is offering them up. The thought of these guys literally eating one of their own made her giggle inside.

She rolled up to Kim Chee's shack and hadn't made it out of the truck before he was standing there, very excited.

"Ribs good! Very good, very tasty. Come try."

That is excellent news! My plan is working perfectly.

She followed Kim into his kitchen, and her mouth started watering when he opened the smoker. The smell was out of this world. She hadn't intended to try one of the ribs, knowing full well what they were, but after experiencing the aroma, she couldn't help herself.

Kim handed her a rib, and she took a small bite.

"Oh my God! This is fabulous. I've never tasted anything like it."

Kim beamed with pride.

"You have more? I take all."

Jesse quickly inhaled the rest of the rib and wiped her face.

"Yes, yes. Let me show you what I have left. But first, can I take some of these with me? I want to share with some friends of mine."

"Yes, yes."

He quickly pulled the remaining ribs off the smoker and wrapped them in foil for her. He was so excited about getting more of this new meat that he practically danced in place.

Jesse showed him inside the trailer and displayed all the remains of Bobby she was ready to part with, knowing she had to keep some in reserve for later. Kim carefully picked the pieces up, looked at them from all sides, and then put them down, almost as if they were precious objects. He had never seen meat cuts like this before, but that didn't matter. He wanted it. All of it.

"How much?" Kim asked, waving his hand over all the meat.

Jesse did some quick math and gave him a number, which he quickly agreed to. She thought about just giving it all to him but thought that might raise more questions. By the end of the day tomorrow, all traces of Bobby would be gone, and Lucky would have some extraordinary bones to chew on.

With her man-bait now secured, it was off to meet the next mark.

She put in a call to Sana and updated her on the sale to Kim. Sana was as excited as she was and felt great pride that their plan worked well.

An hour and a half later, her target came into view. There was still evidence of a fire, and the front section was still boarded up. A couple of pickups and an old Jeep were in the parking lot at the back of the store. She did a slow drive-by and then headed down the street to the new store.

She parked in the corner of the parking lot, as far from the entrance as possible, to keep curious eyes off her rig. As she stepped inside, the smell of everything "packaged" assaulted her senses. She couldn't put her finger on it exactly, but there was a definite smell to these kinds of stores—a sickly sweet combination of fresh plastic, monosodium glutamate, cooking oil, and air fresheners. The scent of those "Evergreen" air fresheners was still overpowering, even through the cellophane.

With a bottle of water and a pack of beef jerky, she made her way to the counter and started her recon.

The bleach-bottle-blonde girl behind the counter was definitely a product of her environment, easily tipping the scale at 350 pounds and reading the latest "50 Shades of Whatever" book—paperback, of course.

Kim would go crazy with all your delicious goodness.

"Hey, I've got a bunch of meat out in my rig I need to unload before it goes bad. Is there a local barbecue joint or diner I could call on? I'd make them a good deal on it," Jesse said, trying to make conversation.

The girl looked at her with the most exasperated look she could muster and said without words: *Why are you botherin' me? Can't you see I was just gettin' to the good part?*

She scanned Jesse's water and jerky.

"The only barbecue thing I know about is the grill the guys next door have on the loadin' dock. They cook up stuff over there every now and then, although it smells sometimes like they're just using it to burn things. Between you and me and the counter, those guys over there are shady, so consider yourself warned."

Jesse tried to give the girl her best "concerned" look.

"Okay, wow. Thanks for the heads-up. You take care."

Hopping back in her rig, she drove down the street and slowly headed back to the loading dock. The big loading bay doors were closed, but the regular exit door was propped open. She circled the rig around, so she was facing out and pulled up just around the corner of the store.

Walking up the dock stairs, she heard several voices coming from inside the warehouse.

"Hello? Is there anybody here?"

The voices suddenly stopped talking, and after a short beat, she heard footsteps heading her way. The two guys, clearly the lackeys, were in their mid- to late-twenties, while the leader seemed to be older, maybe in his early thirties.

The apparent leader of this motley crew spoke first.

"Hey, darlin'. Are you lost or somethin'? What can we do for you?"

"No, no, nothin' like that. I stopped by the store next door and asked the gal there if she could steer me to a barbecue joint or a diner where I could unload some meat that's about to go bad. She told me you guys grill out sometimes here on the loadin' dock, so there you go. Can you help a girl out? I'll make you a sweet deal on it."

Then she squirmed suggestively in her Daisy Duke cut-off jean shorts and black tank top.

"I tell you what, I'll even let you sample it. Follow me."

The guys looked at one another, flashing their most sinister smiles, and followed her outside. When they saw the mobile butchery, they didn't know what to make of it.

Jesse popped open the back of her rig, gathered the ribs Kim Chee had cooked, and passed them to the leader.

"Here, wrap your lips around these. A good customer took these from the smoker just a couple of hours ago. They're mighty tasty."

The leader passed them around. Yummy sounds quickly followed.

"See, I told you they were good. So, can you help a girl out? I'll make it worth your while."

At this, she gave the older guy, whom she assumed was her target Nate, a smoldering look. To verify that, indeed, she had the right person, she introduced herself.

"Oh, I'm Roxy, by the way," and reached out her hand.

"Good to meet you, Roxy. I'm Nate."

Jesse smiled. *Bingo!*

She could tell his wheels were turning about how to get rid of the two lackeys, and almost as if she suggested it to him, he turned and ordered them back inside.

"Why don't you guys go back inside and finish what you were workin' on while I settle up here with Miss Roxy."

Obviously disappointed, they strolled back inside. Then Nate turned back to Jesse.

"Okay, Roxy, show me what you have packaged up in there, and we'll see what kinda deal we can reach."

Jesse hopped back up in the rig and invited him inside. He stepped in and took a quick look around. Feeling alone with Jesse, he reached back, pulled the gate closed behind him, and turned to meet Jesse's gaze.

"I wouldn't want anyone to interrupt our business."

Jesse smiled.

"Absolutely not."

At this, Nate's eyes sparkled with fire.

"So, are you gonna show me what you got, or do I have to pay first?"

Jesse smiled her most devastating smile at him.

"Oh, honey, I think you'll be good for it."

She stepped back slowly and pulled her tank top off, revealing her well-toned torso. Then, seductively, she reached out and slowly wrapped it around his head, blindfolding him.

"Come on now. Is this any way to treat a customer? I like to see what I'm gettin' for my money."

As he reached up to remove the blindfold, Jesse put the C-bolt against his temple, pulled the trigger, and "THWACK," Nate was no more.

"Bet you didn't see that coming, big boy," Jesse said.

As she pulled her tank top free, she noticed Nate's one-eyed ring-neck trouser snake poking up past his droopy waistband.

"Aww, Nate, that's so sweet. Was that for me? You ass wipes always get overconfident when your pecker starts thinking."

She pulled her tank top back on and attached Nate to the grappling hooks with the winch. She slit his throat, thinking he could bleed out upon returning to town. Then, she hopped out of the rig and shouted so the guys inside could hear.

"Thanks, Nate. It was great doin' business with you. Take care."

Seconds later, she was on her way with the package secured.

Jesse texted Sana.

"Package secured. Heading back now."

Sana went to find Anne and Tara and shared the update. They decided to wait together until Jesse returned. It was the longest thirty minutes they had ever spent. When Jesse's rig rolled past the shop window, they walked out to the alley to greet her.

Jesse hopped down from her truck, and the girls all hugged her. Then, looking about carefully to ensure no one else was around, she opened the rear gate to reveal the prize.

After a moment, Anne gasped when she saw Nate hanging there.

"Oh God! That's not him. He's too young. He looks kind of like him, but he's too young. Maybe that's his son. Oh, God!"

Jesse and Sana were stunned.

Jesse said, "What do you mean that's not him? He was exactly where you said he would be. He acted exactly like we thought he would. He even told me his name was Nate, for Christ's sake."

Sana jumped in the trailer, checked his pockets, pulled out his wallet, and revealed his name was indeed Nate. But it was Nate Jr., not Nate Sr.

Tara said, "Lord, ain't that some shit? Well, we can't very well put his ass back together now, so we might as well dispose of him like we planned."

Anne was visibly shaken.

"Oh my, this is bad! What have we done? What have we done! Is this some sick religious karma?"

Sana remained calm.

"Okay, let's look at it like this. Now we know there are two Nate's. We jus' happened to take out the wrong one first. If we had gotten the older fucker first, this asshole would have come around eventually, lookin' for revenge. So, nothin's changed. The plan just got bigger, is all."

Tara agreed.

"You two go do what you need to, and when you're all finished, we'll regroup. In the meantime, Anne and I will work at the church dinin' hall, same as always," Tara said.

"What do you mean, 'Work at the church the same as always?' How can you be so cool and collected about all this? We are in terrible, terrible trouble," Anne said.

Sana wrapped her arms around Anne, who was visibly shaking, and spoke the truth about the consequences.

"Anne, like you said the day we told you about our situation, these people are evil. And they been gettin' away with all manner of nasty shit forever and ever. These are not people the law will be interested in findin'. The people they run with will never report them missing. They'll try and handle whatever happens themselves, just like all the other bad shit they do. Look around this room—if you were one of those bad guys, would you think twice that we might be the cause of their concerns? I don't think so. So, we still have the advantage. We are one up on the score now since Jesse took out a player we didn't even know we had to concern ourselves with.

We got this, Anne, but we must be cool. Can you be cool?"

Anne looked at her with deep concern etched on her face.

"I can be cool. Yes."

Sana released Anne and hugged Jesse, who was still somewhat shocked at the turn of events.

"Come on, girl, we got work to do."

They hopped in the truck and drove away. Tara and Anne returned to the church and pretended all was right with the world.

Sana was constantly amazed at Jesse's resilience. She could tell Jesse had already moved on from this setback and was working on the next take-down—no need to ask—the new plan was appearing undeterred.

CHAPTER 30

Anne replayed the gruesome scene she'd witnessed in the trailer when she learned Jesse had killed the wrong Nate. The shock of seeing a human being hanging like a side of beef, regardless of how evil they might be, was enough to set her off. And when she realized it was the wrong person, it shook her worldview. She couldn't help but feel it was some test in which she had failed miserably.

Her faith in humanity and herself had been slipping for a while. And her conversation with Sana and Tara convinced her that conviction and faith would achieve only so much. Ultimately, she had to work hard and produce her own outcomes, not just "pray and hope" things would work out. Any divine intervention would be her design, not some unseen benevolent force.

And now this has happened.

She paced inside her home, talking to herself, trying desperately to diffuse her rising panic. The rooms felt too small, and the air was suffocating. The daylight streaming in the windows seemed dark, lacking warmth and vitality, almost unhealthy and accusing.

How did she get here? Why did she get here? Had sharing her past with Sana and Tara been a mistake? Should she have shared her entire story with Sana and Tara, not the sanitized version she had contrived for the rest of the world all those years ago?

Anne was just days away from graduating college and felt like letting her hair down. For Anne, this amounted to simply going out instead of staying in her room and studying all the time. A friend had told her about an organization at school—The Baptist Student Union—and they were having a "social," as they called it, which sounded utterly harmless and, therefore, perfect for her. So she made herself presentable, steeled her will, and found her way to the BSU.

When she arrived, she was a stranger in a strange land. She knew not a single face. And even though she was a Baptist, the shenanigans these people were involved with seemed wildly out of place.

Then, a handsome boy caught her eye, and just as she turned away, he approached her.

"Hi, I'm Stan," he said.

"Hi, Stan. I'm Anne," she said, chuckling under her breath at the rhyming of their names. "It looks like you have quite the turnout. I've never been to one of these before."

Stan smiled an uncertain smile and said, "Yeah, we always tend to have a big crowd for the last 'social.' People have been working hard all semester, so it's time to let our hair down. Can I get you something to drink? We have punch and beer if you're of legal age," he laughed.

"Oh, the punch would be great. Thanks."

Stan left to get the punch as Anne walked around. She felt oddly out of place, but then again, she never went out, so the night was a triumph already in her eyes.

Stan gathered up two drinks and looked at Anne across the room. He returned and handed her the drink he had moments ago doctored with an "easy lay" roofie. "Cheers! Here's to new experiences."

"Thanks! Cheers!"

Within minutes, Anne started to feel as if the room was spinning. She'd never been drunk before but felt this must be what it was like.

Stan watched her stagger around with a knowing look and offered to take her somewhere so she could lie down until she felt better. They entered a room at the back of the BSU, where a single-bed cot awaited. Stan sat her on the bed and then sat next to her. Her arms felt as heavy as lead. All she wanted was to lie down. Then, sensing the moment, he gently pushed her down on the bed and pulled her dress up. Anne was barely aware of what was happening, but she knew it was not good, even in her current state. The ensuing date rape altered her life from that moment forward. She had no memory of events after drinking the punch. She didn't even remember how she got home. The one thing she did know with certainty was that she was no longer a virgin. She was so embarrassed by the ordeal that she wanted to forget and move on with her life. But fate had other plans.

She endured all the shame and duress of bringing the baby to term and giving it over to the boy's family. Then, as if God said, "Hey y'all, watch this," ended it all tragically. It was too much. All those lives lost, and so many others ruined, and to what end? What lesson was there in such cruelty? What kind of God puts people to such a test?

But, try as she might, Anne couldn't easily walk away from a lifetime of sacrifice and dedication to this God she had now started to second-guess. It took years of ritual and practicing "her faith" before she had developed even a semblance of meaningful conviction. And even then, when her faith was most vital, there was always a lingering doubt. Maybe her faith wasn't strong enough. Perhaps it was her fault, and she was missing the message somehow. And here was this unavoidable doubt again, making itself known at the worst possible time.

Sana and Tara had shared their experiences with her, which helped her realize she was only fooling herself with the beliefs God might provide. Where was God when that maniac attacked them in their own home? The old saw, "Ours is not to question the will of God," she now conceded, was complete bullshit. It was blind faith that had gotten her into this mess. *She* had to supply the answers. *She* had to find a way to make things right. Not God, not anyone else.

So, now she had come full circle in her thinking, and she felt better about where she was going. Significant setbacks had occurred in her life, and this business with Nate Jr. was not a big deal. Sure, she was complicit in a murder, but only if they got caught. She also felt she would be complicit by doing nothing to bring these terrible people to bear for their actions, especially now that she knew of a way to make significant and permanent changes. Direct and ever-lasting changes.

CHAPTER 31

The mayor sat in his corner booth and chatted with the waitress while he waited for Nate and William to appear. William was first on the scene, so he and the mayor had a few minutes to catch up the situation before Nate broke through the front door.

"Bring me up to speed on this do-gooder," the mayor said.

"Well, she runs a shelter/kitchen operation at the Baptist church in the next county over. Her name's Anne Madison. Our man, Nate, apparently popped in unexpectedly and freaked out one of her women staying there. I don't know what Nate's connection is to this woman other than that she was one of his dimwit runners wife, a guy named Bobby, I think."

"Where is Bobby now?"

"That I don't know, and it's not my problem. That's our man Nate's crew, so hopefully he can tell you."

Nate came through the front door, looked around, spotted the mayor, and walked back to meet him. He did not look happy to be there.

"So, why am I meetin' you here on such short notice? What's the big fuckin' emergency?"

Nate always felt he had better odds if he threw the first punch, even if he was involved in a gunfight.

The mayor sipped his coffee.

"It's good to see you, too, Nate. I'm happy to see you're getting along so well."

William smiled and looked away but didn't say a word.

"I've received word that you've been stepping out of bounds a bit and just wanted to give you a chance to clarify what exactly you're doing. Maybe we can help you; one hand washes the other," the mayor continued.

Nate looked confused.

"What do you mean 'I stepped out of bounds?' And whose word is reachin' your ear?"

The mayor nodded at William, signaling him to tell their friend what they knew.

"I had a visit today from Anne over at the Baptist Church. She said you visited one of her women staying at the shelter. She was distraught by the whole affair. Somehow, she knows about the DG store and that you are running a gang here. She even knows your name. So, that, my friend, is why we are seated here. Now."

After he said this last bit, William's face took on a markedly dark mood.

Nate regrouped but still blustered on.

"Yeah, I went there to talk with one of the women. She's the runaway wife of one of my guys, Bobby. He's gone missin'; he just vanished. And he's not the only one. Another of my guys, Jeff, did the same disappearin' act. I figured maybe she knew where he was."

"Yes, we know about Jeff and have tied off any loose ends there."

Nate looked surprised.

"Loose ends? His old man is in the pen. What other string is there?"

The mayor looked at him until it finally registered in Nate's brain.

"Oh shit. I didn't know. That's above my pay grade, I guess," Nate said.

"Well you guessed correctly. Give the man a prize," William said.

"It looks like you need to focus on getting new runners instead of harassing old ex-wives and do-gooder churchies. Nate, we've got a nice little operation going here, so don't jeopardize that. Keep your crew quiet and your eyes open. I sense these guys who have gone missing are not coming back. That can only mean one of two things: they ran away of their own accord, which is highly doubtful, or someone took them out nice and neat. I'm bettin' that's what we're dealing with now. So, then the question is, what's the threat? Another gang trying to move in? Or something else?" the mayor asked.

Nate and William just looked down at the table in silence.

"I haven't heard anythin' about another gang, and there's no new product popping up, at least none that we've seen, and I feel pretty damn sure we'd know if that was the case. My guys might not be the smartest fucks standin', but they know the street," Nate said.

"Well then, that leaves us dealing with a very different situation: the unknown," William said.

He turned to the mayor for confirmation.

"Okay, we have our marching orders. Let's clean this up and move on."

And with the ease of a practiced politician, he slid out of the booth, shook both their hands like they were best buds, and headed out.

Nate looked at William, wanting to pummel him about the head and shoulders.

"You keep an eye on that church bitch, and I'll get my ship in shape. I don't need you and that fat fuck gettin' all up in my shit again."

William raised his head and looked coldly at Nate but didn't speak, only thinking: *Man, you are one stupid individual. That 'fat fuck' is the only reason you have a business.*

He slid out of the booth and left Nate with the bill.

CHAPTER 32

Secure in their work location again, Sana and Jesse made quick work of Nate Jr. Neither spoke as they worked. There was a solid connection; they considered words unnecessary. Jesse marked, and Sana cut. Sana trimmed, and Jesse packed.

After they finished, they sat out under a shade tree and decompressed. The baby had been very active during the work, but somehow it seemed different, with an "other" quality to its activity. Sana wasn't sure what this "other" feeling was, but she kept trying to pinpoint its meaning.

Jesse finally broke the silence.

"I'm sorry I messed up with young Nate there. Thanks for coming to my rescue with your reasoning. I guess I was just taken with the moment and never dreamed there could be more than one fucker named Nate. And hanging out at the same fucking place."

"No worries. As I said, we would've had to deal with him sooner or later. But now that he's gone, old man Nate will be much more aware of anythin' unusual. If there's one thing we learned with Jr., they both like to take advantage of women, especially women they see as easy targets. That's hard-wired and won't change, even if his radar is lookin' for it."

"How do you think the mayor's involved in this? Is he running the show, using his connections to keep things quiet? Or does he have a bunch of lackeys, like our Nate's, doing all the dirty work? And what about that editor character? There's somethin' off about him. The whole thing is like a loose string on a rug. You start pullin' at it, and the next thing you know, the rug is gone, and all you have left is a pile of string."

"Just keep askin' those questions. Or better yet, take a stab at some answers, and then let's work on plans usin' that. Even if we're wrong, it moves us from where we're stuck."

Jesse looked at her with newfound respect.

"Sana, you're a tough little cookie. You don't let shit get you down. You just keep plowin' ahead."

Sana smiled.

"That wasn't always the case. For most of my life, I was too terrified to think about bein' tough. My mom was like a magnet for the worst kinds of men, and I seemed like an equally strong magnet once they saw me as part of the equation. So, rather than plowin' ahead, I just kept my mouth shut and did whatever they said, thinkin' that might save me some pain, but that shit never worked out either. They beat on me anyway, just for the fun of it. But all that changed the night Jeff came to the trailer. You were there, at least in your vision. If Mom had been off just a fraction of an inch with that shotgun, my head would've been all over the ground. That broke somethin' loose deep inside, and I ain't ever goin' back. Shit got really clear after that. I don't know whether it's this demon seed inside me or somethin' else, but whatever it is, I'm gonna ride it as long as it'll run."

"Yeah, that scene with Jeff was something. Do you think we'd see a different vision now if I put my hands on your baby?"

"I don't know, but I can't see how tryin' would hurt. The baby was active while we were workin' on Jr., but it felt different somehow. I can't put my finger on it. Maybe Nate hadn't reached his most awful self yet, so the baby didn't react strongly. Who knows?"

Jesse turned and faced her, and Sana followed suit. As Jesse touched the baby, it kicked to life, surprising them both. She closed her eyes and made the connection.

As her mind's eye opens, Jesse sees herself on the runway at Bouncing Betty's. It's amateur night, and she's shaking her money maker for one audience member only: Nate, Sr. He eyes her with sinister intent. The two lackeys are there as well, watching from the bar. The scene changes. Nate is hanging up naked in the trailer, screaming in pain. His lackeys are hog-tied and watch in terror. Jesse is asking about Anne and Beth. She calmly asks Nate, "Where are they?" His stalling is rewarded by Jesse popping the side of his ankle with the C-bolt. Nate screams, "F-u-u-u-u-c-c-c-k! You fucking cunt!" Jesse bends down so she can whisper in Nate's ear, reaching down and grabbing his cock and balls in her hand as she does. She raises the C-bolt, presses it against his scrotum, and says, "You got to three. One... two..." Stop!"

Jesse takes her hands away from Sana's belly.

"Oh shit, Nate Sr.'s is going to kidnap Anne and Beth! Our brilliant plan has me dancin' at a strip club to lure him in. You're there, as are the two lackeys I saw earlier. There was somebody else I didn't recognize, but he seemed part of our gang—a big guy who knew the lackeys. We've got to stop him."

"What the... Well, that's easier said than done. We can't watch them both 24 hours a day. And his lackeys would recognize you from before. I think I know who the big stranger might be. He might be the key to breakin' this thing up. Before we get too carried away, though, let's share what we think we know with Anne and Mom."

"Okay, let's get out of here."

CHAPTER 33

Beth could tell these guys would cause trouble as soon as they entered the dining hall. She didn't know who they were, but she recognized their MO. The skulking way they walked, glancing around to see who was paying attention to them, with hands tucked in their pockets. She thought about bolting for the door, but it was too late. They recognized her and were walking straight towards her.

"Hey, Beth. What's the matter? Not happy to see us?" Lackey 1 asked.

"You wouldn't happen to know where Bobby is? He hasn't shown up for work in a few days. I hope everything is okay," Lackey 2 smiled.

"I don't know where he is and couldn't care less, so why don't you just leave me alone?"

"Come on now, is that any way to talk about your lovin' husband? He was always so generous, sharin' you with friends and all. It hurts me to hear you talk about him like that," Lackey 1 said.

Beth was furious but also very scared.

"Look, I left Bobby weeks ago, just after your boss paid me a surprise visit. That's the last I've seen of him."

"It's funny you mention the boss. He sent us to check on you and your friend here at the church. It seems she's been talkin' to some folks and gettin' herself into some troublin' stuff. And it looks like Nate Jr. has gone missing, too, just after the boss last saw you. That seems like a strange coincidence to me. How about you?" Lackey 2 asked.

"Please, just leave me alone. I have nothing to do with whatever you're talking about."

"The boss said he'd like to talk with you, but not here. It seems your friend doesn't want him comin' around. So, come with us, and everything will be fine," Lackey 1 said.

"No, I am not leaving with you. No way!" Beth shakily said.

"Oh, I'm sorry. Did you think we were asking? My bad. Let's go bitch! Now!" Lackey 2 said, grabbing her arm and twisting it hard.

She knew better than to scream or make a scene, so she did as they asked. As they walked down the street, Beth looked all about her, trying to find an escape. Just as they were about to shove her into the back of their SUV, she spotted Sana and a stranger coming down the road in big rig. Sana spotted her, so Beth squirmed just enough to let her know there was trouble. Just as she spotted Beth, the lackeys spotted Roxy.

"Hey, isn't that the gal who popped by the warehouse the other day? What was her name? Roxy?" Lackey 1 asked.

"That's her alright, and that big fucking rig of hers. I don't recognize the other gal. Tell me what you're thinking."

"Let's hang here a sec. I want to talk with her. She's the last one who saw Nate. Maybe she knows where he is."

Beth was confused, knowing it was Sana in the rig, not Roxy. She kept quiet and hoped the girls would try to help her somehow.

As they rolled past, Jesse spotted the two lackeys.

"Oh shit! That's the two fuckers who work with Nate Jr.," Jesse said.

"And it looks like they have Beth. Shit!" Sana said.

"Pull around back and I'll see if Anne's in the church," Sana said.

"Okay. I'll drive back around and see if I can engage them. You watch out from the church. I'll stay in my truck if they try to get all handsy."

"Girl, are you crazy? What do you mean by 'engage them?' They'll recognize you for certain."

"I'm hoping that's the case. They seemed disappointed the other day before I took Nate Jr. off the board. He told them to get lost while he had his way with me. Maybe I can use that to my advantage. As far as they know, Nate was okay after I left; he just wasn't there."

"Be careful."

Jesse pulled back around the church and slowed as she approached the lackey's SUV, rolling down the passenger side window.

"Hey, guys. I thought I recognized you. How are you boys doing?"

"Hey, Roxy. We're doin' okay. What are you doin' in these parts?" Lackey 1 asked.

"Oh, I'm headed out to the country to see a client about some cows. I picked up a hitchhiker on the road and dropped her off."

"If you've got a sec, we'd like to talk with you about our friend Nate. It seems he's gone missing, and you're among the last people who saw him," Lackey 2 said.

Jesse put on her best "concerned look" face, thinking: *No fucker, I was the last person to see him.*

"Oh no! I'm sorry to hear that. He seemed pretty happy when I left him at your place. Maybe he got all spontaneous and did a beach run or something like that."

"Maybe. Anyway, if you could spare a few minutes, our boss would make it worth your while," Lackey 1 said.

Jesse looked at her watch.

"I'd love to help, but I can't be late for this meeting. I tell you what, though: tonight is 'Amateur Night' at Bouncing Betty's, and I was thinkin' of trying my luck on the runway. I know it's hard to compete with the workin' girls from the other clubs, but I figure nothin' ventured, nothin' gained. Maybe I'll see you there," she said, winking at them. "Bring lots of singles now, as that's how they chose the winner. You boys could help put me over the top."

"Well, alrighty then. We'll see you later," Lackey 2 said and smiled.

Beth had no idea what in the heck just happened, so she kept quiet, hoping there was a plan in there somewhere.

As Jesse pulled out of town, she called Sana and told her about the plan. Like in the vision, she would dance tonight at Bouncing Betty's and felt sure Nate Sr. and the lackeys would be there.

"I haven't found Anne yet, so I don't know if she's safe. I'll meet with her friend David and see if he can help us. He knows these guys from workin' on their trucks and can help us deal with them at the bar."

"Sounds good. I'll think about how we get Nate Sr. under control. I'll check back in later."

CHAPTER 34

Nate Sr. looked at himself in the mirror and was pleased with what he saw. The brown uniform and cap would be enough to fool that bitch of a church do-gooder into thinking that he was just another harmless delivery guy. And while his van didn't exactly look like a UPS truck, he didn't feel that would be a problem either. He'd park out of sight and walk up to the front door. Picking up a package along the way would also be no problem. Drivers left boxes in plain view all the time. It was almost like they were daring you to steal them.

He went out to the warehouse for an update on Beth.

"Do you have the camera set up on the girl? I want to test it out before I hit the road."

"Yeah, Boss, all you have to do is dial the number, and I'll answer the call. FaceTime will do the rest. Give it a try."

Nate dialed the Lackey's phone, and he answered on the first ring. He had to admit that the cameras on these new phones were the shit. Even though she was in a dark room, her fear was loud and clear. The fact that she was hanging upside down and gagged with duct tape helped.

"Perfect. Beth, you hang in there. I'm going to get you some company real soon," Nate said.

As he drove to Anne's house, he continued to sort out what he knew and didn't know about the recent disappearances.

The girl, Jesse, had shown up at the DG just before Jr. went missing.

The do-gooder had started digging around the story on the DG at about the same time.

Could they be related somehow? He didn't see any connection, but he wasn't concerned. He'd grab the woman and bring her back to the warehouse. From there, things would either get better for her or much worse. The choice was hers, as he was just the delivery mechanism.

Finding the do-gooder's house was simple enough. He just had to wait outside the church until she left and then follow her home. He returned the next day and cased the house while she was at church. There were no signs in the yard that indicated an alarm system. She didn't have one of those fancy doorbell cameras, which he was genuinely thankful for. There was no big dog, only an orange cat. Perfect.

As he pulled into Anne's subdivision, he started looking for a package to steal. Bingo! A small box was on the front porch of a nearby neighbor, just calling his name.

He parked the van, hopped out, and pulled his hat down. The clipboard made him look somewhat official. He picked up the package, checked a box on his clipboard, and headed back to the van.

Then he rolled slowly down the street to the large hedge that separated Anne's house from her neighbors and parked the van. He hopped out and dialed Lackey's phone.

"You set?" Nate asked.

Beth's terrified face came into view.

"Yep. Good luck."

"We won't need any of that. This bitch is all but in the bag."

Nate approached the house with his cell phone on his clipboard. To Anne, it would look like one of those devices delivery people use to make you sign for packages.

He punched the doorbell and waited.

After a short while, Anne looked through the sidelight on the front door. She opened the front door but kept the glass/screen door closed.

"Can I help you? I wasn't expecting any packages today."

"I'm sorry, maybe I have the wrong house. You recognize this person?"

Nate held up the phone so Anne could see and hear Beth. Beth tried her best to scream but could only make a terrified whimper.

It took a moment for Anne to recognize what she was looking at, and during that time, Nate pulled out his pistol and pointed it at her.

"I thought I had the right house. Let's step inside for a moment, and we'll get this delivery all sorted out."

Anne thought for a second that she should slam the door shut and call the police. But then she thought of what might happen to Beth and decided to let Nate in and see where this would lead.

"You've been snoopin' around my business a little too much lately, and my folks don't like that kind of attention. So, we'll take a little ride and see if we can sort all your questions out. Grab your phone and purse like you're goin' to work, and we'll walk out of here. My van is parked just around the corner. Remember, my friend here will have your back the whole time, so don't think about makin' any kind of break for it. That would truly be bad for your health. Got it?"

"Yes, yes. Just don't hurt Beth."

"She'll be fine as long as you do your part. You both will, you'll see."

Nate helped her into the van, and they returned to the warehouse. Anne sat as quietly as a church mouse the whole way and kept playing David's warning about Nate repeatedly in her head.

As the warehouse came into view, Anne's worry ratcheted up.

Nate pulled around behind the store, and a large garage door opened. He pulled inside, and the door closed behind them.

All types of shipping boxes and palettes were inside the large space.

Nate hopped out and was greeted by two lackeys. They were both armed with what looked like assault rifles.

"Take Anne in there to see her friend. Do everything you can to make them comfortable."

The lackeys laughed in unison.

"On it, boss. Right this way, please."

They lead Anne down a short hallway to a darkened room.

They flipped on the lights, and Anne saw Beth strapped down on a stainless-steel table. Her mouth was still duct taped, and it was clear she had been crying a lot. There was another table right next to her, which Anne correctly assumed was for her.

"Beth, it's going to be okay. We must be smart, and it will all be okay."

"Okay, smart lady, you see how this is supposed to work. Lie down real still on the table there, and like you said, everything will be okay," Lackey 1 said.

He zip-tied her hands and feet to each corner of the table. She was face down on the table, which significantly increased her discomfort. Her field of vision was minimal.

"Okay, I'm going to take this tape off your mouth so you and your friend here can catch up. But if we hear any nonsense from you, we'll tape both of you up. We'll be listenin' in, so don't say anythin' that might hurt our feelings. We're kind of sensitive about that kind of stuff."

They left after tying her to the table. Switching the lights off plunged them into pitch-black darkness.

"Beth, are you okay? Besides tying you down on the table, did they hurt you in any way?"

"No, thankfully, that's all they've done so far. I'm so sorry you're in this mess. I should have run away at the first sign of trouble. I'm so stupid!"

"Beth, stop talking like that. You did nothing wrong. If anything, I made this worse with my snooping around. I'm sorry we're both in this predicament, but I'm not sorry I stirred their shit up."

"How are we gonna get out of here? No one knows where we are."

"I'm not sure, Beth, but we have to have faith that somehow, some way, our friends are going to try and find us."

And it will be horrible when they find these fuckers.

CHAPTER 35

Sana filled Tara in on the situation on the way to see David. She could only shake her head and say, "Oh my! Oh my! Oh my!"

Sana hoped David would be willing to meet them at the club and distract the two lackeys so Jesse could focus her attention on Nate Sr.

They stopped in his driveway and, as they walked into the shop saw half of him hanging out from under a car.

"Hey, David. It's Sana and Tara. We hate to bother you, but we really need to talk with you."

"I'm kind of busy here, ladies. Is there something wrong with your car or what?"

"No, no, the car is doin' great. We're just concerned about Anne. I think she came to see you about a guy named Nate. Well, we think he might have taken her. Have you seen or talked with her today?"

David came flying out from under the car on his creeper.

"No, I haven't talked with her since the day she came and asked me about Nate. I told her to be careful with that fucker. What makes you think he's involved?"

"Well, when Jesse and I were pullin' into town today, we saw his two lackeys with Beth, a friend of ours from the church, and it was pretty clear it wasn't a friendly visit."

"How do you know these guys are his lackeys? It could be just two random guys."

"That's a story for another time, but trust me, I know these guys are connected to Nate," Sana said.

"Okay, so what do you need from me?"

Sana brought him up to speed on the plan for later that night.

David's part would be to keep the two lackeys occupied at the bar while Jesse did her tricks on the stage for Nate. Jesse may also have something else for you to take care of since this is a 'work-in-progress' kinda thing."

David looked very concerned upon hearing this.

"This Jesse sounds like quite a character. How do you know you can trust her? And what does tonight have to do with getting Anne back?"

Tara said, "David, we love Anne, just like you, and want to find her before somethin' terrible happens. You need to trust Jesse to deliver Nate. I don't know how and don't need to know how, but I'm gonna trust she can do it."

"Okay. When should I plan on meeting with you guys beforehand? I assume you don't know me from Adam once we're inside Bouncing Betty's. I want to meet Jesse beforehand to see what she has up her sleeve."

"Thank you, David, thank you. Give me your cell, and I'll text with a time and place after I talk with Jesse again," Sana said.

Back in the car, Tara now had a list of questions.

"How we supposed to take out three men and three bad men at that? I know I sounded all confident back there with David, but I think you gals are stone-cold crazy if this is the best plan you can work out."

"Mama, you know that vision I told you about when Jesse was with us and Jeff at the trailer? Jesse and I tried somethin' this mornin' after disposin' of Nate Jr. She wanted to see if we could conjure up another vision by touchin' my baby, and it worked. Jesse saw this whole night play out in her vision. David was there, although she didn't know who he was, along with Nate Sr. and the two lackeys. I won't go into all the details, but she has a plan. Undoubtedly, shit could go sideways in a hurry, but that's a chance we have to take."

"Like they say, 'Better the devil you know.' What we gonna do?"

"I'm not sure. The lackeys saw me with Jesse, and she told them I was a hitchhiker, so I'm not part of the plan, or that might trigger something. We'll have to hide somewhere at the club until Jesse and David come out with their peeps."

Sana called Jesse back.

"Hey, where are you?"

"I'm on my way to see my barbecue guy. I hadn't planned to meet him again so soon, but now that I have an extra body packaged up, I need to make space in the freezer for later. Plus, I needed to clear my head for a bit and work on this plan. What's up with David? Is he in?"

"Yes, he's in. Like us, though, he's concerned about all these moving parts. He wants to meet beforehand and go over everything. When and where is a good spot?"

"Let's meet back at the salon at 5:00. That'll give me time to make the drop and get back to town with a clearer plan. Cool?"

"That works. I'll call David. Good luck."

CHAPTER 36

Anne awoke with a start and tried to look around the darkened room. She had gone to sleep, which seemed insane to her. Her mouth was duct taped now, and her hands and feet were still zip-tied to the table. The coolness of the stainless steel on her cheeks made her prone position even more uncomfortable. She could hear a lot of activity on the other side of the wall. When she tried to raise herself to change position, the ties cut into her wrists and ankles, making things worse.

Beth could hear Anne moving around on the table nearby and tried to communicate, though she was also duct taped.

The darkness made every sound more terrifying than it otherwise might have been.

Nate and the Lackeys watched them squirming on the monitors in his makeshift office. The night vision mode of the cameras gave the whole scene a sinister look they loved. Nate was in no hurry to talk with them. He'd let the darkness loosen them up a bit.

After what he felt was a suitable amount of simmering, he flipped a switch, and music started blaring. The combination of jet-engine volume and the screaming voices rattled their ears. It wouldn't take much of this before they would be deaf.

Then, the sounds changed to roaring chainsaws and blood-curdling screams. At first, they thought it was coming from the speakers, but then they smelled the smoke and realized the sound was in the room.

Suddenly, a spotlight shone down on them, blinding them. When their vision settled down, they saw a lone figure with the chainsaw dressed head-to-toe in a hazmat suit. Covered with polka dots. WTF?!

He held the saw over his head and revved the engine, filling the room with blue smoke. Then he swiped it down along the table's edge, sending sparks shooting into the darkness.

Then the room was plunged into darkness again as the sounds echoed away and silence returned.

The sound of the girls hysterically crying replaced the noise. After a few moments, they settled down, feeling like maybe the worst had passed.

Then, they heard the mechanical sound of a hoist pulling up the foot of each table until they hung vertically a few feet off the floor. All the blood rushed to their heads, and the pain was excruciating as their total body weight pulled against the zip ties.

The tables started swaying slowly back and forth as the hoist tracked back and forth above them. They heard Nate start singing.

"Rock-a-bye baby, in the treetops."

As he got to the last bit of the first section of the lullaby, he screamed into the microphone, "And down will come baby, cradle and all!"

Just as quickly as it started, they were plunged back into complete darkness and unearthly quiet again. They could only hear the ringing in their ears. They hung suspended for what seemed like an eternity. Then, without warning, they were lowered back down. Their fear now was what was waiting at the bottom of this descent.

Nate turned and looked at the lackeys.

"That, boys, is how you put the fear of God in someone. We'll let 'em think the worst there in the dark until we get that Roxy gal."

"She'll be really easy to spot at Bouncing Betty's. When they start the amateur night part of the show, she'll be on the stage in all her glory. After the show, we'll snatch her in the parking lot, sweet and simple like that," said Lackey 1.

"We'll give you the nod when she's about to start so you can get a front-row seat," Lackey 2 said.

"Sounds like a plan. We'll bring her back here and add to our drama. Then our show can begin. Let's head out," Nate said.

CHAPTER 37

When Jesse arrived at the salon, David and the girls were talking. She reached out and shook David's hand.

"Hey David, I'm Jesse. Thanks for agreeing to help us out with these assholes."

"I just hope you know what you're gettin' into. These are not your garden-variety, bad guys."

"Thanks for the heads up, but just so you know, we aren't your garden-variety vigilantes, and I've got a freezer full of body parts to prove it."

David's eyes widened, but he kept quiet. He focused intensely on Jesse as she laid out the plan.

David's role was to distract the two lackeys, buying them rufie-laced beers at the bar. When they went down, he and Tara would drag them out to the trailer and tie them up, hog style. Then, they were to come back inside and wait for a sign from Jesse on Nate. She didn't know what that would be, but they'd all know when the time came.

Jesse would center her performance on Nate. Knowing he couldn't control his misogynist nature; it was simply a matter of pushing the right buttons at the right time. A suggestive wink, a flash of hot pink, and a whispered invitation are all it would take. His arrogance would deliver him to the slaughter.

David thought: *Damn, this girl is shithouse-rat crazy. Hotter than fuck, but crazy.*

"Where do you want me?" Sana asked.

"I think you should be our eyes in the parking lot, watchin' out for anybody we don't suspect. Call David if you see someone who looks like trouble, and he can decide what to do."

"Jesse, you sure you want to go through with this shit? There's a whole lot of places this thing can get sideways," Tara said.

"This is our best chance. We know Nate has Beth, and since we can't find Anne, we have to assume he has her somehow. If he's as bad as David says, and I believe he is, there's no time to waste. I'm counting on their arrogance and confidence. They'll underestimate us, and that'll be all she wrote. I guarantee it."

"David, she's right. These assholes are used to folks like us bein' afraid of them. They'll never suspect anythin' until it's way too late. And if they do, we'll improvise. We know their goal is to snatch Jesse. They don't know our goal is to take them. And when they see what lies ahead of them, they'll be scared shitless. We'll give them plenty of chances to believe they can talk their way out of it, but in the end, they're goners. It's a matter of how far down pain's highway they want to travel," Sana said.

David was getting more nervous by the minute.

"Okay, let's head out. I'll see you guys tonight. Be ready."

Jesse checked herself into the nearest motel she could find.

She made herself irresistible to Nate, shaving everything baby-butt smooth and rubbing herself with lotion. She checked her tramp stamp tattoo in the mirror. It had several honeybees circling a hive. "Honey Hole" was tastefully rendered in a wedding invitation script underneath.

Nice!

Sana and Tara made ready, trying to stay as calm as possible. The baby, however, was having none of it. It was more active than ever. The only time it settled down was when conversation stopped around the plan. The more Jesse talked about what they were about to do, the more excited it got. Sana hoped and prayed that all this excitement wouldn't result in an early appearance by the little devil.

"I'm gonna bring somethin' extra just in case that sideways shit you mentioned happens," Tara said.

Sana knew what she meant and nodded. "Good idea."

David had similar thoughts as he drove back to his garage. He would bring several insurance bits ranging from a .357 snub nose pistol to brass knuckles and a Billy Club. *You never know what kind of fight you might get into, so like a good Boy Scout, I'm gonna be prepared.*

100% BOTTOMLESS GENTLEMEN'S SOCIAL CLUB
XXX
BOUNCING BETTY'S
· SINCE 1971 ·

SO
EASILY
LEAD

CHAPTER 38

It was just about 9:00 p.m., and things inside Bouncing Betty's were jumping. Amateur Night always brought out a good crowd. All the leering locals who'd seen the regular gals a thousand times wanted some fresh meat to come into view. Not that they had a clue what they would do with it other than look at it.

Nate and his lackeys arrived right on time. David spied them as soon as they set foot in the bar. He waited until they had seated Nate next to the runway. Then, as they approached the bar, he caught their eyes and invited them over for a beverage. They gave Nate the thumbs up, and he waved them on.

David greeted them like long-lost buds.

"Well, look what the cat dragged in. How are you boys doing?"

"Hey man, we're doing good. Hope you are. I didn't expect to see you here," Lackey 1 said.

"Hey, I may be old, but I ain't dead, at least not yet." He waved to the bartender, "Get my boys here two tequila shots and two beers."

"Thanks, man," Lackey 2 said.

"So, what brings you boys out tonight? I do hope you're not going to get up on that stage. I'm not sure my eyes could take a site like that."

"Aw, fuck you, old man. I'd look better up there than your big gorilla ass. At least I got some moves," Lackey 1 said, gyrating his hips as David hid his eyes.

The drinks arrived, and David proposed a toast.

"To new meat! Cheers!"

The lackeys threw their shots back, sucked their limes, and drank a deep swig of beer.

Betty took to the runway with a microphone in hand.

"Give it up for all the ladies. They all work so hard for you."

A smattering of applause rippled through the bar.

"And now, what you've all been waiting for. Time to crown a new Miss Erotica."

A loud whoop and holler went up in the bar.

"That's more like it."

Then, looking back to the end of the runway, Betty winked for the first contestant to come out.

"Please give it up for Tessa."

There was mild applause as Tessa made her way onto the runway.

She was pretty in a traditional sense but a far cry from anything exotic or erotic, dressed in what looked like an everyday sundress. The bump-and-grind music surprised her, and she slowly started rocking in place. After a bit, she pushed her dress off her shoulders, letting it fall to her waist. A nice pair of pert tits greeted the audience, who responded halfheartedly.

It was clear to all that Tessa was not enjoying this, and as she tried to up the ante by stepping out of her dress provocatively, she caught her foot and stumbled, almost falling off the runway.

There was a small roar of laughter and boos as she quickly gathered herself and left the stage in tears.

Betty tried to hug her as she ran past.

Betty came back out to introduce the next act.

"Let's give Tessa another round of applause."

A couple of working girls clapped, but that was all.

"Next up, we have the amazing Roxy."

The spotlight followed Betty back to the end of the stage, then went dark for a beat.

Jesse burst through the curtain when it popped back on, dressed in her most erotic lingerie and spiked heels. She had heavy, smoky eyes, the whites of which seemed to peer out of a black cauldron.

There was a roar from the crowd. This is what they all came to see, and she wasn't about to disappoint.

As she broke through the curtain, all heads turned, and David saw his chance to tweak the lackeys' drinks. Plop, plop, gone, gone.

Jesse did a series of very acrobatic moves, stepping out of her heels, cartwheeling down the runway, and ending up right before Nate, all in one graceful motion.

Dropping seductively down on her hands and knees, she spun around and hung her leg over the edge of the runway to entice him a bit, and as he reached up with a single, she slid her other well-toned leg over his shoulder.

The crowd went wild as she glided back on stage.

She ripped her lacey bra off at the end of a pirouette, hurled it at Nate, and landed it perfectly over his eyes. Tinsel tassels on her perfect tits began spinning in unison.

Back in front of Nate again, she bent over double and looked at him through her legs. Back to a standing position now, she slowly tugged her lace panties down, rocking them side to side, revealing her "Honey Hole" tramp stamp.

She turned and winked "goodbye" at Nate as she flashed her hairless girlie-bits at him.

He's mine now.

As the music wound down, Jesse returned to the stage entrance, the crowd going wild, yelling, "More, more, more!"

Betty bounced onto the stage.

"I think we have ourselves a winner already. What do you think?"

The crowd went even wilder.

Betty called out to Jesse.

"Roxy, get back out here! Your audience awaits!"

Working the crowd like a pro now, she glided down each side of the stage as hungry patrons rushed to the runway, shoving their hard-earned Washington's and Lincoln's into her garter.

When she returned back around to stand beside Betty, it looked like she had two greenback wreaths wrapped around her legs.

Nate reached up to hand her bra back, grabbed her arm, gently pulled her down, and whispered.

"Roxy, that was quite something, especially for an amateur. Won't you join me for a drink? I promise I'll make it a night you'll never forget."

Jesse smiled, retrieved her bra, and whispered back.

"Sure thing, sugar. Let me get my stuff from in the back, and I'll come find you." Winking as she strutted away, she said, "Don't go anywhere."

Nate nodded and smiled.

As he waited, he looked around for his guys. They were nowhere to be seen. *They must be in the head or something.*

David led the two lackeys outside the bar towards Jesse's trailer. As the drugs kicked in, he had to carry them for the last few steps. Sana came over to help him.

"How's it goin' in there? Your part worked well. Did Jesse get Nate's attention?" Sana asked.

David dragged the two inside and hog-tied them.

"Oh, she got his attention alright, him and everyone else with eyes. Shit, there isn't a limp dick in the place."

Sana couldn't help but laugh.

"Okay, way to go, Jesse. So now we wait, right?"

"Yep, now we wait. I've got a feelin' it won't be long."

David hopped down and shut the trailer door.

As Jesse made her way back to Nate's table, she noticed the lackeys were gone, as well as David.

That leaves just you and me, Nate.

Nate stood as she reached his table and, putting an arm around her, guided her to her seat, holding a small gun against her ribs.

"Well, friend, is that a warm gun I feel all nice and hard, or are you just excited to have a drink with me?"

"You think you're something, don't you? I must admit that the show you put on was very entertaining. I can't wait for an encore performance back at my place. My boys must have found some friends somewhere, so you and I will take a little ride together. We have some things to discuss that I'm sure you'll enjoy."

Jesse eagerly slipped her hand up Nate's leg, rubbing his inner thigh, testing his willpower.

"Oh, baby, I'm sure I will. There's no need to be so bad with the little shooter. I'd rather play with your big gun."

She licked her lips suggestively as she stood to go.

As she stepped outside with Nate, she stretched her arms over her head, as if she was being held at gunpoint by a bad guy, and inhaled deeply.

"I just love the feel of cool, crisp air on my skin. It makes all the good bits so sensitive."

Then, as she brought her hands down to her side, distracting Nate for just a tick, David came out of the shadows, smacked him on the back of his head with a Billy Club, and ducked back into the shadows for cover. Nate didn't make a sound as Jesse caught his fall, laughing as if he had stumbled from too much drinking.

"Oh, baby, baby. I told you not to have that last shot. You gotta learn some limits."

Looking around the parking lot for wandering eyes, she staggered towards her trailer. Sana quickly joined in, opening the gate, and helping her inside, and David closed it all up again, quick as a bunny.

Once inside, Jesse quickly hooked Nate up to the wenches.

First, she attached his hands to each end of a long metal bar, stretching his arms out as far as possible.

Next, she pulled him up as his knees barely touched the floor and ran a short cable across the backs of his knees.

Then, she attached another cable to his feet and winched them back, so it started to cut into his knees.

The whole affair looked like a kneeling Jesus on the cross when finished.

Jesse drove out to a different secure location with the three packages.

David and Sana followed behind in their cars, creating a caravan into the country. Twenty minutes later, they could move on to the next phase: information extraction.

CHAPTER 39

"So, how is this going to go, exactly? You plan to threaten him somehow to get information? I'm not sure that's gonna work with an asshole like this guy," David said.

"Oh, he's a slippery fuck, no doubt. And that shit with the gun was unexpected, especially right there in the bar like that. But let me tell you, this fucker has never seen anything unexpected like what we're about to show him. I'll put more than the fear of God in him. He'll pray to the Devil before I'm finished with him."

Sana looked at David and shook her head in the affirmative.

They opened the gate and stepped inside.

Nate was awake and moaning in pain. The lackeys were also awake and looked terrified, as they knew where they were: in the butchery trailer. Nate had yet to learn this juicy news.

He tried squirming free but realized that wasn't going to happen.

"Damn you, bitch. Get me down from here. What the fuck?"

Jesse grabbed him by the head and turned it hard to the side so he could see his partners hog-tied on the floor. He realized he was truly fucked now, but he had no idea exactly how fucked that would be.

Jesse spun him back around so he could see her plain.

"Here's how this is gonna work, Nate. Pay close attention now because it's slightly different than what you might do."

She reached up, grabbed her C-bolt, walked past Nate, and stooped in front of one of the lackeys on the floor.

"For example, if I was in your situation, this is where you'd threaten me with bodily harm if I didn't answer your questions."

Then, as casually as swatting a fly, she pressed the C-bolt to Lackey 1's head and pulled the trigger.

"THWACK!"

Lackey #1 was dead, with a freshly punctured hole right in the center of his skull.

"That sound never gets old. I love it!"

It took all the intestinal fortitude he could manage for David not to run outside and throw up.

Sana's gaze was stone cold. Her baby was doing back-flips inside.

Jesse returned to where she could see Nate's eyes.

"So, because I'm a kind-hearted gal, I'm gonna ask my question just once, really nice. And if you don't answer it quickly, the lovely me you see here leaves the trailer, and my evil twin comes in and takes over. Trust me, you won't like her very much, I guarantee."

Nate struggled to no avail.

"Where do you have Beth and Anne?"

Nate was surprised by this question because he had no idea how Jesse was connected to those two. He tried a bluff.

"I don't know who you're talkin' about. What makes you think I have them anyway?"

"Oh well, I guess it's time my evil twin took a swing at you. She'll be right in. Don't you go anywhere."

Jesse stepped into a small room at the front of the trailer and stripped down to her thong and sports bra. Then she donned her special strap-on dildo/C-bolt with the fillet knives in the holsters. Standing upright after tying the blades snugly around her legs, she checked herself in the mirror. *Show time!*

She stepped back into the trailer where Nate was hanging.

Walking behind him, she stooped down and shot the C-bolt through the side of one of his ankles.

Nate screamed out, just like in the vision.

"F-u-u-u-u-c-c-c-k! You fucking cunt!"

He didn't know pain could be this bad without dying, and this new information scared him even more.

Jesse stooped down again so she could look into his terrified eyes and asked as calmly as a child, asking about a friend.

"Where are Beth and Anne?"

Nate held out, hoping for some Divine intervention.

"I told you; I don't know who you're talkin' about."

Then, she kneeled and reached her hand deep into his pocket as if searching for his car keys, grabbed his balls, and started twisting. To make sure she had his attention, which she felt was extremely hard to get, with the other hand, put the C-bolt against his penis.

"Maybe this head is better at rememberin' things. You got to three. One..."

Nate struggled through the pain to speak.

"No, please, no!"

"Two..."

Finally, Nate relented and started talking.

"Stop! Stop! They're at my store, where you met my son. They are fine; I swear it on my mother's grave, they're fine."

"I'm always surprised at guys like you and how you let the little head take things over. That little noggin cares about only one thing, and trust me when I tell you, it's not your well-being."

She motioned for everyone to step outside so they could regroup, and she could get some clothes back on.

David was utterly out of his element with all this.

"What the fuck was all that? I thought you would smack them around a little to scare them, not just off them like that. Holy fuck!"

He frantically rubbed his scalp as Sana spoke.

"I'm sorry, David. If we'd told you what we intended, you probably wouldn't have helped us. You'd have said, 'Go to the cops' or offered some other useless advice. Cops don't give a shit about people like us. They don't even see us. If you want to bug out now, we won't stop you, but we could still use your help. Anne and Beth could use your help. Once we get them safely back in our care, you can forget this whole mess, and Jesse and I will take it from there."

"Okay, okay. Let's make that happen now. How far away is this place?"

"It's the next county over, so about 30 minutes. Follow me," Jesse said.

The caravan regrouped and headed out.

CHAPTER 40

Anne and Beth were left alone and in the dark. After all they'd been through, the comforting quiet was a welcome relief. But when they heard vehicles approaching, they started to freak out again.

"Anne, what will they do to us now?" Beth asked.

"I don't know Beth. I'm hoping and praying that the girls pulled off a miracle and are coming to save us. I'd stopped believing in miracles, but these last 24 hours have renewed my faith. I hope it's not misplaced."

Then they heard voices coming. Anne imagined it was David yelling her name. Was her mind creating what she wanted to hear, or was he really here? The overhead lights flickered on, and she saw three people running toward her.

Sana stooped to see Anne's face.

"We're here, Anne. We got you!"

Beth started crying as Sana freed her hands and feet.

"Sana, thank God you're here. Please tell me that awful man is gone."

David quickly cut Anne free and reached down to help her sit upright on the table. She immediately threw her arms around his neck and almost strangled him, hugging him hard.

"David, thank you so much for saving us. I've always said you were a Godsend. Now, do you believe me?"

David hugged her back.

"If you say so, who am I to argue?"

Beth started screaming.

"I said, tell me that awful man is gone! Is he dead?"

Jesse went to her and wrapped her arms around her, comforting her.

"No, Beth, not yet, but he won't ever hurt you again. We have him outside. They're all outside. I thought the two of you might like to speak with him before he goes away."

Beth broke free and started running for the door. Everyone followed, catching up to her as she reached the trailer.

"Where is he? Is he in there? Show him to me!"

She was moments away from a total meltdown.

"Hold on, Beth, we have to do one thing first. David, get that roll-up door raised. I want to bring the trailer inside so people can't see what we're about to do," Jesse said.

David ran to get the door, and Sana led Anne and Beth back inside.

Once the trailer was inside and the door closed, Jesse opened the trailer and turned on all the interior lights.

When Beth saw Nate strapped in place and blood running down his body, she froze momentarily. Then the damn burst, and she lunged into the trailer, kicking and punching him for all she was worth, screaming at him. Catching her breath, she noticed one lackey still alive and started in on him, venting her unbridled rage. After a few minutes, Beth collapsed on the floor and sobbed, her body shaking.

Anne stepped into the trailer and comforted Beth for a moment.

She turned and faced Nate, who, miraculously, was still conscious.

"I have some questions for you before Jesse has her final say over you."

Nate groaned but could muster little else in protest.

"What's your connection to the mayor? He owns this store and the one down the street, so I'm assuming you're running some shady operation out of here for him."

Nate didn't respond, so Jesse intervened.

"Nate, Anne asked you a question. And she did it much nicer than I would have. I suggest you answer in a like manner. Now!"

Then she grabbed the C-bolt and popped his other knee. After he stopped screaming, Jesse nodded for Anne to continue.

"Anne, ask Nate your question again."

Even after all Nate had done to her and Beth, she was still shocked at how ruthless Jesse was in dealing with him.

"Who else is involved with your operation? Is the editor at the paper part of the plan?"

Incredibly, Nate held out, but when Jesse stepped forward again, he finally broke.

"Yes, yes, yes! They're all involved! The mayor buys the drugs, using his contacts in other countries, and runs them through here. He's a pharmacist, but as dirty as the day is long. When that reporter came snoopin' around after the fire, he caught the scent of what we were into. Sensing an ongoing cash stream, the editor extorted and blackmailed the mayor. His insurance policy is a fully-baked story that drops if somethin' happens to him."

"Nate, you guys need to stop watching the TV so much. That little situation you just described happens in EVERY FUCKING CRIME STORY! I'm so disappointed in your complete lack of creativity. Honestly, I expected more," Jesse said.

"I'm with you. Why should we believe such a boilerplate setup? I hope you have something to back that up."

Nate croaked, spitting blood out of his mouth.

"It's in the safe, in my office—all of it. Cut me down from here, and I'll open it for you. Promise."

Jesse laughed at him.

"Nate, my man. There is no promise you could make that's gonna get you down from here. You stay here and think about how you want to spend your last few minutes while we check this out."

David and Sana ran towards what they took for his office. It didn't take long to locate it—the old "behind-the-fake-panel-in-the-bar" trick.

David grabbed the safe with his big meat hooks and yanked it free from the wall. Then, looking around the office, he noticed the chainsaws Nate had used to terrorize the women earlier.

"I got this." He fired up one of the saws and let the sparks fly. In a few minutes, the door dropped away. There was the usual collection of cash and ledgers inside. David raked it all into the trash can and returned it to the trailer.

Sana dumped the contents on the floor, where Nate could see them. As he realized his last card, the old "I'll unlock it for you if you cut me down" card, had been called, what little color he had left drained away.

"Which ledger has the blackmail contents?" Sana asked.

Nate realized now his time was short, so he decided, as his final act of defiance, to fuck the mayor and the editor over but good.

"It's the one with the yellow 'Smiley Face' sticker."

Anne quickly grabbed the ledger and checked the entries. It was all there. This scam had been going on for years. All those lives these fuckers had ruined with their poison. And she felt more than confident that he would have killed her and Beth if Jesse and Sana hadn't intervened.

Nate tried one last Hail Mary.

"I gave you what you wanted, so cut me down. We had a deal, right?"

Then, when he thought the worst was over, Jesse grabbed a bottle of

Jack Daniels and took a deep swig. Then she splashed some in Nate's face, burning his eyes.

"You fuckin' bitch! I gave you everything you asked for. What are you doin' that for?"

Speaking very calmly again, Jesse grabbed Nate's head in both hands and said, "Oh, sweetie. We moved on from that interrogation a while ago. I have to say, you did very well, although you were a little stubborn there for a bit. Now, we're onto a completely new line of questioning. Do you remember visiting Bobby's wife at his apartment and collecting what he owed you from her?"

Nate looked at her, even more terrified.

"I'll take that look as a definite 'Yes.' She told us how kind and gentle you were with her. So, we thought it was only fair and right to repay that kindness to you now. You ready?"

Nate struggled as best he could, but the cables were more than a match for his strength.

Jesse splashed more Bourbon in his face, then roughly grabbed him by both his ears and twisted them for all they were worth. When his mouth flew open in a scream, she shoved the dildo/C-bolt in as far as she could.

Beth looked on with fire in her eyes.

"Oh yeah, I do believe you've done this before!" Jesse moaned.

Nate had tears running down his miserable face as Jesse skull fucked him for all she was worth.

"I can see how a guy might like this kind of thing. I mean, I have total control over your worthless ass right now, and I must say, it feels pretty damn awesome."

Nate moaned.

"Oh, do you need another drink? Okay, here you go."

She poured the rest of the bottle over his face, almost making him gag.

Then, Jesse started thrusting again.

"Okay, I think I'm about to have that Holy O! Wait for it!"

She thrust even faster, harder, and then, pretending she was about to come, hit the trigger, and the C-bolt shot through the back of Nate's head.

Then she stood quiet and still, catching her breath after all the exertion. "That's for wastin' all our time, fucker."

Even though Jesse had just put Nate down, hearing his last ploy put Anne over the edge. All the suppressed rage she felt from women coming to her at the church boiled over. The pain they endured. The shame they suffered. The futures lost. She'd had enough and decided not to turn the other cheek again, not this time. She grabbed the C-bolt from Jesse, bent down, and shot Nate right between the eyes again.

"Thank you for that, Anne. Thank you," Beth said.

Jesse looked at Sana.

"Okay, girl, are you ready to get to work?"

Sana looked at the remaining lackeys.

"What about him?"

"Oh, I think our boy here likes to watch, so let's oblige him before we pack him up for Kim Chee. Cool?"

"Yes."

Her baby kicked wildly.

CHAPTER 41

The evening air outside the trailer was cooling down from another scorcher. A gentle breeze swept across the pasture while the soft sounds of cows mooing in the field supplied a nice bass line to the cicada's high-pitched trill. A pack of coyotes, a.k.a. "Song Dogs," bayed in the distance. The moon was the kind Emmylou Harris might sing about as a bunch of cowboys sit around the campfire eating beans and breaking wind.

For the next several hours, the girls worked methodically and intensely. Jesse kicked on some heavy metal tunes, rocking and swaying to the beat while she hacked and sawed. There was a fire in her eyes that Sana had never seen before, and once again, she was glad to know Jesse was on her team.

The overhead LEDs lit up the inside of the trailer, throwing everything not lit directly into harsh shadows. Knives, cleavers, and saw blades of every description hung on long magnetic strips just above the counter. Jesse kept the saws and other power tools stored in the deep pull-out drawers below the counter-top area—a place for everything, and everything in its place.

Raw blood and other body fluids swirled aimlessly around the shallow stainless-steel sink to the right and drained into a holding tank below.

They had tucked the heads, hands, and feet away in plastic barrels filled with a salty brine mixture, to be processed later into animal feed.

A high-pressure spray nozzle was neatly coiled at the end of the trailer, making it easy to hose down the entire trailer interior when needed.

The baby had been overly active, but Sana had grown used to that. It seemed to enjoy the carnage as much as Jesse did, maybe more.

They had almost finished processing the second lackey. Sana had made all the heavy cuts, so it was a matter of trimming some fat here and rib cartilage there, wrapping it all up, and they'd be good to go. Nate and the first lackey were already wrapped and stored in the freezer. All in all, an excellent yield. Kim Chee would be so excited.

Stepping back so she could survey the counter, Jesse noticed something alarming, turned to Sana, and said, "Whoa, girl! Holy shit, you've got a lot of blood running down your legs there! You've got to be more careful not to get that shit on you. There's no telling what kind of germs these crazy fuckers might be carrying."

Sana powered down her saw, flipped her blood-spattered face mask up, looked down at her thighs, and realized the bloody mess was coming from her, not the body on the counter. She hiked up her work apron, looked more closely, and saw a mixture of sticky fluid and fresh blood.

"What the... Oh shit, that's coming from me! Oh no, I think my water just broke!"

Then, as if she'd flipped the main switch on a power station, she started cramping for all she was worth. She staggered back against the trailer wall in pain and slid down to the floor.

"Oh my God! I think this little devil is gonna make his appearance tonight. What the fuck are we going to do?"

"WHAT?! We're too far away to drive to a hospital, and besides that, we can't risk someone seein' what we've got goin' on in here."

"OH GOD! This shit hurts!"

Sana felt a popping sensation, and then her water broke in full, flooding the trailer floor with blood and amniotic fluid.

Jesse looked at her with fear in her eyes and said, "Oh shit, Sana, it's game on now! I'll go get some blankets out of the truck."

The urge to start pushing was overwhelming, but Sana had no idea if that was good or bad. The pain consumed all the available reasoning power that remained.

Jesse quickly returned with the blankets and worked to make Sana as comfortable as possible.

"I got you some water. Here, can you take a drink?"

Sana grabbed the bottle and took a long drag until a cramp took hold of her body again. She dropped the bottle, and it rolled across the floor.

"Okay, I'm gonna take a look down there and see if I can tell what's goin' on," Jesse said, as if she had some idea of what she was looking for.

She helped Sana slide her blood-stained panties off, and Jesse could see her cervix was already starting to crown.

"Oh my God, I can see what looks like its head starting to push out! This little fucker is in a hurry."

"OWWW! What the hell! It feels like I'm trying to push a basketball out of my hoo-hah!

Sana started taking very shallow breaths. The cramps helped in this regard, as they were coming so fast she didn't have time to breathe. Then, the urge to push overwhelmed her. She balled her fists, closed her eyes, and pushed for all she was worth.

"Okay, it's moving, it's moving. Don't forget to breathe!"

"OWWWWW!"

"Shit, its head is already out! Holy shit, holy shit! Hold on, let me grab it! Wait, it's got the cord wrapped tight around his neck! What do I do with that? What do I do!?"

Sana tried to catch her breath briefly, but the baby thought, *No way, I'm out of here.*

"Okay, its shoulders are out." The baby practically shot out in the time it took to say that. "Holy shit, he's out! It's a boy! It's a boy! What do I do about this fucking cord?"

"Cut it! Cut it!" Sana yelled.

Jesse reached up and grabbed her favorite knife off the counter, splashed some fresh water across the blade, and cut the cord all in one fluid motion.

"How does he look? Is he breathing?" Sana asked.

"He's purple and covered with goo! Don't they always slap their little behinds on TV shows? Should I do that?"

"Yes!"

Jesse held him up by his tiny feet and slapped his little behind. The first time, nothing happened, so she hit him harder, trying desperately not to lose her shit. Finally, the baby started to cry.

"OKAY! Okay! He's breathing! He's breathing!"

Jesse handed him to Sana, who was covered in sweat and exhausted. She held him close to her breast and wiped some of the white goo off his tiny body with her shirt. He whimpered a little and instinctively started looking for her nipple.

Jesse laughed. "That little guy knows what he wants, and he knows how to get it. That's amazing."

She collapsed on the floor opposite Sana and started crying. The tears were a mixture of exhaustion, stress, and personal grieving for the child she lost long ago.

"Jesse, thank you so much for helpin' us through this god-awful mess. There's no way I could have done that without you."

She crawled across the floor, wrapped her arms around them, and hugged them as she continued crying. Sana could tell tears of joy were mixed in there, but she could also sense her grief.

"You're so welcome, Sana. I've never been so afraid in my life. Thank God we didn't have any more surprises than we did."

Jesse fell back against the opposite side of the trailer again, and they both caught their breath. She didn't realize how exhausted she was until she felt sleep trying to creep in.

"Hey, I'm really wiped. I'm gonna take a quick power nap, and after that, I'll get us squared away, and then we'll get the fuck out of here. Cool? Are you and the baby gonna be okay for a bit?"

"Hah, I think we'll be okay. At least I know how to reach you if we need anything. Sleep well.

EPILOGUE

Anne looked out over the crowd in the dining hall. Nothing much had changed as far as these poor souls were concerned. They were still oppressed, hungry, and suffering. But in her soul, Anne knew the world was a better place because of what they'd done. They had removed several evildoers and perfected a system to take care of many more. A sense of profound justice replaced any guilt she might have had.

"Hello, Mr. Mayor, this is Jim Rice, a reporter with the Times. I want to ask you some questions about your alleged involvement with a large drug enterprise recently uncovered in your county..."

Upon hearing the words "large drug enterprise," the mayor's mind shut down, and all he could hear was a high-pitched whine in his ears.

"Mr. Mayor, are you there? I need to ask you some questions."

"I'm sorry. I think it's best to contact my lawyer. Thank you," and he hung up.

How in the hell did they connect me to this debacle? Even he didn't know what happened when the whole thing went to shit. Everyone just disappeared without a trace. The only sign of trouble was the apparent break-in in Nate's office, but he couldn't see how that connected him in any way unless that rat bastard had some evidence he was holding to use himself at some point.

He called the editor at the paper to see if he had heard anything. It automatically went to voice mail, something that had never happened before. Not good.

Meanwhile, the editor was having his own fun time in the barrel. He had managed to duck the calls from reporters, but when the Feds knocked on his door, he knew it was time to look out for number one.

Fuck the Mayor. It's every man for himself now.

As he opened his front door, the agent said, holding up his badge, "William Morrow, I'm with the FBI. You're under arrest for connection with…

Jesse never dreamed this new product would be as successful as it was. Kim Chee couldn't get enough. Word spread around the area, and soon, others like him started asking when and where they could get some of this fabulous new meat.

As a bit of a lark, she updated the advertising graphics on her trailer, adding pictures of Jackalopes and Unicorns with big headlines for her new "Unicorn Ribs" and "Jackalope Sausage." She even developed a new product out of the skins they had to remove from their chosen ones— "Rascal Rinds"—her take on the ubiquitous pork rinds. Drop them in the deep fryer for 30 seconds, and viola, "Rascal Rinds." Crispy!

Sana and Tara settled into a routine at the salon. She kept the baby, Damien, in a little bassinet in the corner so she could keep an eye on him. He was pretty good most of the time. The only exception was when one of the new ladies would start dumping their bucket of woe from the salon chair. The more dire their story, the more agitated Damien became. Sana began referring to this favorite toy as "the death rattle" because she knew the next target had been selected whenever he picked it up.

ACKNOWLEDGMENTS

First, dear reader, thank YOU! If you read these words, you have invested valuable time in my latest enterprise. I hope you felt like it was a good investment.

I want to thank all my "Early Readers," Jill LaForge Jones, Jay Fields, and, particularly, my wife Fran, for their feedback and support.

Thank you, squared, to Richard Norris at Project 13, who brought all his incredible design skills to the book. He embraced the project with a talent and passion that is a beautiful thing to behold.

I'll end where I started. Thank you for investing even a small amount of your valuable time with this cast of characters. I hope they opened your eyes and mind to what may or may not happen in our daily world.

CON
FESS
IONS

FROM THE CHAIR

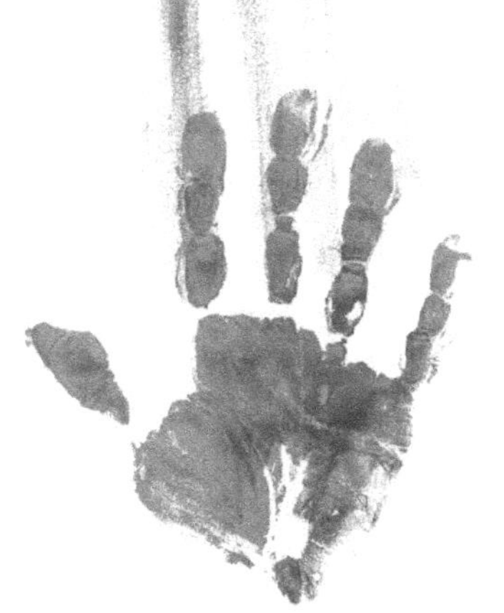

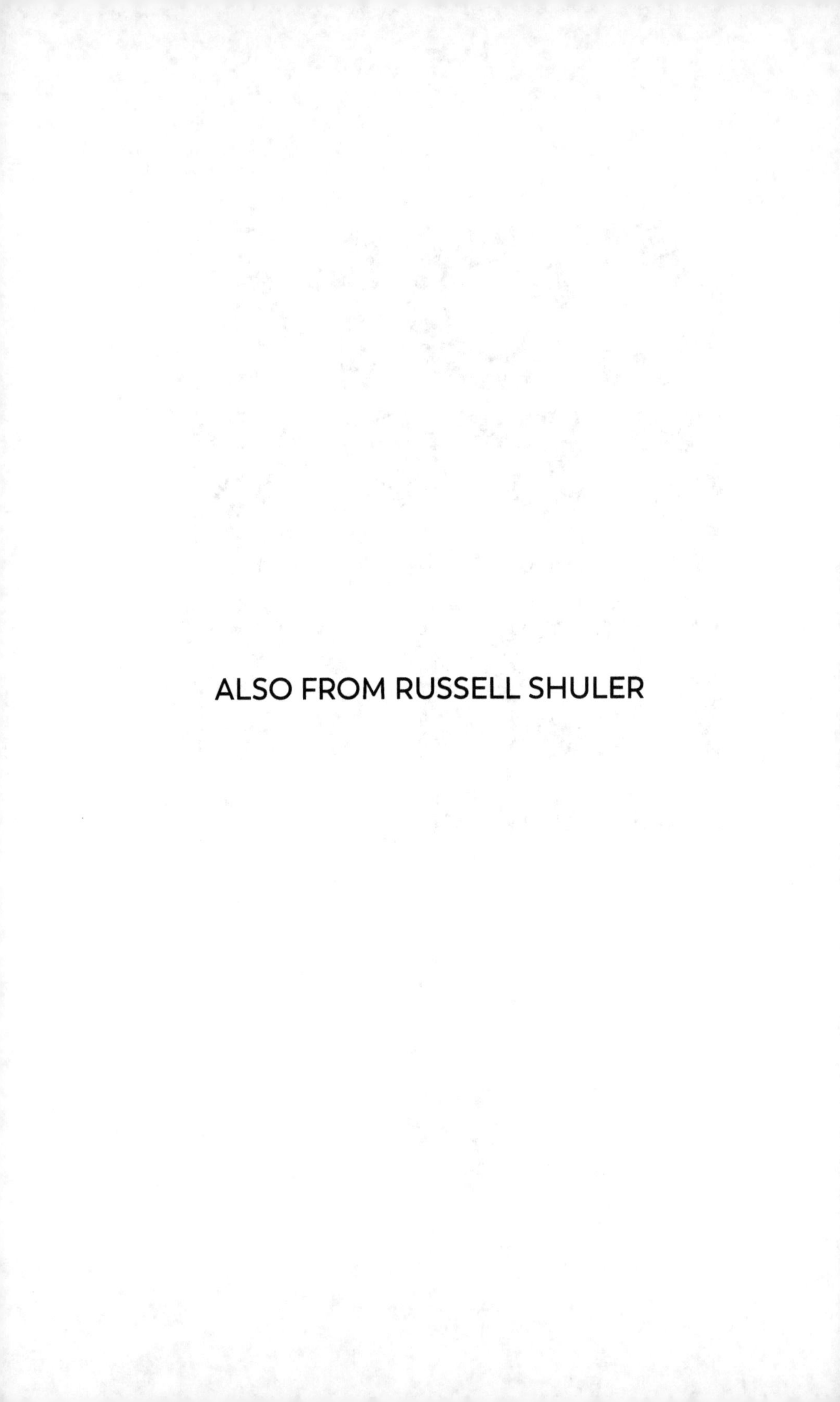

ALSO FROM RUSSELL SHULER

Instant Ancestors

Preposterous tales sprung from a shoebox.

Russell Shuler

Instant Ancestors

The Genesis of Instant Ancestors

It's been said many times that you can pick your nose, but you can't pick your relatives. I believed that to be true until, not long ago, I came across a shoe box crammed with family portraits taken roughly a hundred years ago in a favorite antique store. The stall proprietor included an index card with the scribbled broadside: "Instant Ancestors!" It went on to say that with these pictures, you could conjure up a long-lost relative from God knows where famous for such and such, and no one would be wiser. To be truthful, the idea appealed to my lop-sided, passionate sense of humor, so I bought the box of photographs and began imagining the personal chronicles of these precious folks who had been relegated to the dustbin of history.

Of course, none of the characters I conjured are real, even remotely so. On the other hand, certain sayings and mannerisms flutter into the light of these tales from acquaintances in my past. Sorry about that—it's just that I largely went with zero impulse control in the tales that follow. I can't be held responsible if they resurrect someone buried in the annals of your very own family. And should there be no real likeness to anyone you know, buried or alive, consider yourself one incredibly lucky individual.

– Russell Shuler

Cletus McHaggis

CLETUS MCHAGGIS

"So... are you gonna make a move any time today, or should I come back around tomorrow?" asked Willie.

Cletus answered with nothing more than a squinty stare. It was his not-so-secret weapon, and it didn't matter if he was playing a game of checkers or bidding on a steer down at the stockyard, and if you engaged with him, you were likely to fall victim.

After an uncomfortably long period, McHaggis responded, "When I'm darned good and ready, you'll know." He felt he now had Willie by the short and curlies, just like he liked it.

"Shoot then. I'm out! I can't be dragging ass for days on this chair while you make up your mind about whether to jump me." Wille snarled, kicked the chair over, and shuffled away.

Smiling on the inside, Cletus stared at the board as if carved from alabaster until Willie was out of sight, then intoned quietly to himself, "Gotcha again, you little shit!"

McHaggis discovered at an early age that if you weren't too quick to respond to people, they'd often proceed in the direction you wanted. And it didn't matter what kind of negotiation it was; the method was bulletproof.

Even as a baby bouncing along in a dusty covered wagon headed west with other homesteaders, he used this technique when breastfeeding Mammy. However, he was unaware he was doing so at the time. For example, she'd put her big old jug in his face, and he'd look at her, thinking, "Why do you have that pink-nippled, milk-smelly thing shoved in my face like that?" All of this, he said internally. All his Mammy heard was "Wah! Wah! Wah!" as he stared at her.

He'd continue to use the same gamut eating at the table with the big folk. Then, seeing his empty bowl, his Mammy would ask, "Clete, do you want some more porridge?" Of course, he did, but he wasn't about to let her know it, so he just stared at her for a few minutes. Then, after what became an uncomfortable moment, she'd heap another spoonful into his waiting bowl.

This technique also became invaluable when he started courting young girls. For example, when he and Maggie were rolling in the hay in the old barn, and she started getting as frisky and fiery as her red hair, she would sit astride him and sweetly ask, "Would you like to have a play with my little knockers, young Clete?" Thinking to himself, "What a stupid question. Of course, I'll be wanting to fondle and snuggle my face in your little cleavage and maybe in some other choice areas." But all he said was nothing. He just stared. Granted, it was a curiously intense and wild-eyed stare, but it was a stare nonetheless. Not sensing any reluctance from Cletus, Maggie removed her lacy under things and commenced satisfying her natural inclinations.

This formula of "non-response" responding seemed to have increasing power. The more Cletus didn't react to something and just stared away, the more people did as he wished. It was the darndest thing.

One day Cletus found himself in a bit of a pickle, though, and as you might guess, it involved a skirt.

Her name was Esmerelda, and she was like the famed literary figure in many respects, sans goat. She was a dark-haired beauty of Spanish descent, with eyes as green as the emerald coast of Ireland and dark olive skin. A singing and dancing member of a traveling medicine show. She loved to haggle and barter and was good at it, a traveling carnie her entire life. Moreover, she made exquisite use of her good looks. Purring and circling targets, letting her body do most of the talking as her prey fell speechless.

McHaggis first spied her riding into town, caroling sweetly to herself. He waited on the shady side of the street in front of the saloon. He cast his powerful stare her way, which was usually all he required to attract someone his way, and he felt Esmerelda would be no different. At least, that's what he thought as she pulled her one-horse cart in front of the saloon.

She stepped down from the cart, tied the horse's reins to the rail, dusted off her dark pleated dress, checking to make sure her frilly white blouse was hanging just right off her shoulders, adjusted her corset for maximum bosom effect, turned, and marched his way. Clete had never felt more optimistic about his prospects of bringing a hot-blooded filly under his command; all he had to do was bear down with his long, hard look.

But as she got closer, each step more provocative than the last, something captured his senses. Her fragrance was otherworldy! In a completely uncharacteristic move, he deeply inhaled her heavenly aroma and closed his eyes, almost floating up from his chair. Then, quick as a wink, the advantage shifted in Esmerelda's favor—she sashayed past him directly into the saloon without offering so much as a second glance. That she-devil!

This insult absolutely could not stand. Cletus jumped out of his chair, kicking over the checkers table, scattering checkers all over the street. Then, moving through the swinging saloon doors, he encountered a scene that stopped him cold. The entire population inside the tavern, men and women folk alike, were sitting or standing there, slack-jawed as wayward mules, rubbernecking this raven-haired vixen. The barkeep nervously cleaned a shot glass like his uneventful life depended on it. Finally, the piano player broke the spell when he started tinkling with the ivories, producing a tune no one recognized.

"I would like a glass of your best Madeira, kind sir," she lilted to the stunned fellow behind the bar.

"Ma-what?" he asked.

"Red wine! Like Bacchus pours out of his belly button," she spun as only a cunning temptress could.

"Why didn't you say so then? Sorry, we ain't got no wine. Beer and whiskey is all we pour here," mumbled the keep.

"Then pour me a quick whiskey, you gringo, before I smack your mouth!" she grinned.

Damn! McHaggis had never witnessed such a creature; truth be told, he was fearful about the whole prospect of engaging with her, yet he couldn't help himself. He had to get her attention and level up the playing field. But by what strategy? She was impervious to "the stare." And her anger was quick to rise. So whatever his next move was, he had to be sure, or it might be his last.

In a Fell Swoop

He casually strolled into the bar, never once taking his eyes off her, feeling that to do so would only increase her control. But unfortunately, even the back of her beautiful head seemed to have authority over him. Dropping down on a stool at the end of the bar, he ordered a beer and a beef jerky, thinking they might help stick courage to the post.

"Where are you coming from, lovely senorita?" he asked as gentlemanly as possible.

Looking straight ahead in the mirror behind the bar, she tossed her whiskey back in one fell swoop and said, "Same place I'm headed back to—what's it to you, mister?"

"Hold up! That's no way to treat a fellow, especially when I asked you all nice," Clete retorted, feeling dangled in space. "Here, let me buy you another tipple from the old jug. What do you say?"

Esmerelda turned on her seat to face him and said, "Pardon me, kind sir. Of course, I'll have a drink with you! Who knows what it could lead to?" She giggled, batting green eyes. Then, in a gush, she sauntered down to his end of the bar and nodded to the stunned barkeep.

"Name's Cletus. Cletus McHaggis. At your service, ma'am."

"Cleee-tus! So very lovely to make your acquaintance. You may call me Esmerelda, as everyone does." Then, whispering, she said, "Although a few handsome men have given me other names."

Feeling like he was gaining ground, Cletus sallied forth. "I'd like to propose a toast. To the indomitable Esmerelda and her secrets—may they be revealed to the worthy!"

"Why, Mr. Cleee-tus! You flatter me talking about secrets. I am but a shy, hard-working showgirl making her way in this big lonely world, singing and dancing to bring a moment's joy to people along the way. If those kind souls feel moved to bless me with a friendly word, a tasty meal, or, as you have so gallantly done, a tipple from the bottle, then the world is all the better for it," she exclaimed for all within earshot as she raised her glass.

"Cheers!" rang out across the bar as if she had pulled a puppet string dangling from everyone's back, and their tongues started wagging. The piano player suddenly found his hands again, unleashing a ragtime tune. The mob rushed to the bar like a tsunami to be close to Esmerelda and her intoxicating rapport.

The place surrounded her, everyone shouting and screaming to buy her another drink, a continental drift that filled Esmerelda with glee. Then, quick as a cricket, she jumped on the bar and started to sing and dance, swooping and swishing her long black mane for all it was worth. The piano player did his best to keep up. Everyone juked and jived to the rhythm of the moment.

Then everything got deathly quiet. Esmerelda stopped, tossed her head back in ecstasy, took a bow, stepped off the bar, and waded through the dumbfounded crowd and out of the saloon.

Cletus cautiously followed her out the swinging doors, unsure about his next move. Then, catching up, he escorted her across the street and up to her carriage.

Uncorking an inviting smile, she said, "Thank you kindly, Mr. Cleee-tus McHaggis. Our gang is staying just on the outskirts of town for a few days, and if you were to find yourself out that way for some unknown reason, Lord knows what mischief we might get into."

Swallowing hard, Cletus could only croak, "Yes, indeedy. Yes, indeedy. Good day, my lady."

He watched her leaving town, feeling a deep yearning for the very dust her wagon wheels kicked up. Feeling as if he had fallen into the tail of a random comet ripping across the night sky.

Doppeling the Ganger

When she returned to the Medicine Show, Esmerelda's identical twin sister, Desdomena, greeted her. The two were indistinguishable from each other, even to close family members, a likeness which came in handy when the two bestowed mischief on some poor, unsuspecting soul. Esmerelda hugged Desdomena, and the two climbed inside their covered wagon.

Esmerelda regaled Desdomena with her exploits in town, especially the winding up of Mr. Cletus McHaggis. This man, she felt certain, would be an easy mark, but they would have to plan carefully to bring him to his knees. The two would act like a mythical Janus, with one face setting Cletus up and the other taking him down a curved and humiliating road. Or, so they strategized.

All the years staring people down had taught Cletus one crucial fact: you had to concentrate intensely on what people said and, even more importantly, on what they didn't say. Through critical observation, you could unlock a person's innermost thoughts. This practiced discipline had created his ability to discern refined, almost incomprehensible details. Like how a person looked at you or not. How they breathed. Whether they hesitated at specific points during the conversation, as if waiting for information to fall into place before proceeding. And how was their body language? Did it change subtly from one moment to the next? All these clues painted a picture for Cletus to work with as he moved about his everyday world.

So, in this state of heightened awareness, Cletus proceeded out of town to the Medicine Show. The ride out clarified things to a degree. He had a chance to review the previous day's events, almost like watching one of those new-fangled moving pictures, and he fixed in his mind on as many details about Esmerelda as possible. Hair color and texture. Facial expressions. Eyes, mouth, teeth, everything. She would not catch him off guard again.

It was near dark, the golden hour, when he arrived at the campsite. The carnies had a fire roaring, and his mouth watered at the smell of smoking meat. He could hear someone plucking a guitar in a flamenco rhythm accompanied by a beautiful voice he recognized as belonging to Esmerelda. But, in the air, there were hints of something else: cannabis and peyote. This could get interesting.

"Hola! Welcome, Mr. Cleee-tus, to our humble campsite," came a voice he didn't recognize. It was Juan Carlos, a.k.a. "Sweetie" to family members, walking over to greet him.

"Gracias! Pleased to make your acquaintance," replied Clete, already cataloging Juan's particulars for later usage. "That was some mighty fine playing you were doing there, so please, don't let me stop you."

"You are kind, Mr. Cleee-tus," purred Esmerelda as she joined them by the fire. "Let me fetch you a drink. I hope you like tequila."

McHaggis replied, "I'd prefer Irish whiskey, but if tequila is what you're pouring, I'm obliged to follow your lead."

At this, Esmerelda ducked behind the wagon. Desdomena was secretly waiting there, taking in the conversation. She was dressed as a mirror image of Esmerelda, matching in every way. Desdomena whispered to Esmerelda as she poured the drinks, "So what's the play with this gringo? I'm assuming you want to loosen him up, and then what?"

Esmerelda replied, "I'm still trying to decide what prize awaits us at the end. He carries himself quietly, more steely-eyed than any man I've ever encountered. But we will strike when he feels the need to break his silence and make a move. It's all about timing. That is why we must loosen him up with tequila and peyote first. It will slow his reactions and give us an edge."

Cletus sat near the fire and cataloged the site. He could identify five to seven gypsies, guessing there were probably twice that number. Their wagons were covered with heavy canvas tops and splashed in bright colors with carnival-like markings. The wagon wheels had pinstripes; any sign painter would be proud to call the work his own. Clearly, this was a source of pride for the group.

"Juan, that is a mighty fine wagon you've got there," said Cletus. "Did you paint it yourself?"

"Ah no, that would be Esmerelda's handiwork. She has an eye for such things. Her mother, God rest her soul, was gifted in the same way," he replied. There was the slightest hitch in his response, like he was about to say another name, when "Esmerelda" clicked into place.

Esmerelda returned with drinks and sat down next to McHaggis. The combination of the crackling fire and the early evening sky, combined with the closeness of this fascinating creature, intoxicated the visitor. Any fire the tequila lit would be redundant.

"To our newfound friend, Mr. Cleee-tus McHaggis! May he be found worthy of much and suspected of little," Esmerelda smiled.

"My worth is yet to be determined. But if I am any judge of character, and I like to think I am, I suspect you'll make an appraisal, fair and square, of any values I possess," Cletus winked.

The circling had begun: like two well-seasoned wrestlers facing off in an unseen ring. One looked for innuendo, while the other looked to remain concealed and unsuspected until the jig was over.

After a couple of rounds of drinks, Cletus felt warm and fuzzy all over, but not defenseless.

He began to stare at Esmerelda as a wily crocodile with an extra pair of protective eyelids. And just like a croc, he would lay in wait, staring for as long as it took to disarm his prey, tequila or not.